Laurel's Choice

A Laurel Rowan Story

Nancy M Bell

Print ISBNs
Amazon print 9780228628644
BWL Print 9780228628651
Ingram Spark 9780228628668
Barnes & Noble 9780228628675

BWL Publishing Inc.

Books we love to write ...
Authors around the world.
http://bwlpublishing.ca

I0584396

Dedication

For all those who are open to the beauty and magic of the impossible which is possible

Chapter One

"Laurie? You in here?"

Laurel Rowan sighed and saved the document open on her laptop. "In here." She straightened the papers scattered on the desk before looking up at the tall cowboy in the doorway. "Did you need something, Chance?"

Chance Cullen stepped into the room, hat in hand, a bewildered expression marring his rugged face. "No. I mean yes." His words stumbled to a halt, fingers running around the brim of his black Resistol.

"That's helpful." Laurel leaned back in the chair and rubbed her stiff neck. "Something happen over at the Diamond C Dad needs to know about?" She reached for her phone.

"What?" Chance's head jerked up. "No, everything's good at home." He sought and held her gaze, suddenly annoyed and vulnerable at the same time.

"Then what? I've got a ton of stuff to get through for Dad. All these calving records and then I need to file the registrations for the foals ... so if—"

"Tell me you're not really going," Chance burst out, the long muscles of his neck rippling as he swallowed hard.

"Oh for the love of God." Laurel smacked an open hand on the desk. "I should have known Carly would spill her guts."

"It's true then? You're really gonna go back to England?" Something glittered in his blue eyes.

"It's not set in stone, but yeah, I applied for a working student position with an Olympic Three Day Event rider. I want to come home afterward and go for my Equestrian Canada NCCP Competition Coach Specialist in Eventing. I've already got the Competition Coach English certification. So I guess that means, yeah, I'm gonna to back to Cornwall if they accept me." Laurel let his gaze squarely.

"Awe, c'mon, Laurie. You can do that here. I heard you and Carly talking about it. She's pumped to do the Western levels. You don't have to go all the way over there to get certified to coach." Chance stepped closer, set his hat on a chair, and leaned on the desk with both hands.

"Don't call me Laurie." She ground her teeth and stood up abruptly, sending the chair rolling back against the office wall. "I don't *have* to go *all the way to Cornwall,* you're right. But I want to! I've read a ton of stuff about the program, and it sounds awesome. Not to mention I do have friends in Cornwall I'd like to see."

Chance snorted and straightened up, eyes blazing. "So that's how it is, is it? This is all so you can be close to that English dork, isn't it? Long term relationship not working out so well? Worried he might have something going on the side..." He broke off at the dangerous expression on Laurel's face.

"For your information Coll and I are doing just fine, thank you. Not that it's any of your business. God, Chance, just when I think maybe you're starting to act like a good guy you go all asshat again. Honestly, sometimes you make me want to hit you over the head with something." Laurel broke off and gathered up the laptop and papers. "I'll finish this in the house. Get out of my way."

"Geez, Laurie. Okay, I'm sorry. I was out of line, but Carly blindsided me with the news, why didn't you tell me yourself?" Chance wisely stepped out of Laurel's way.

6

"Why? So you could go sideways on me? I was planning to wait until things were settled and then tell you." She brushed by him and started down the stairs.

"You afraid I'd talk you out of going?" He stomped down the stairs behind her. "It's a big step, Laurie."

She stopped so suddenly he banged into her and almost landed on his ass on the step behind him. "Don't call me Laurie!" Laurel poked him in the chest with her finger. "Honestly, how many times do you have to be told?" She whirled back and continued down the staircase.

"Okay, okay. Sorry." Chance rubbed a hand over his chest.

Reaching the bottom of the steps, Laurel waited for Chance to clear the doorway before closing and locking the door to the office. "For the record," she informed him, "there's no way you could talk me out of going *if* I decide to do this."

"Does that mean you haven't decided for sure yet?" He jammed his hat on his head and waited for her to turn out the barn lights, following her out into the chilly April evening.

"It means I'm still working out the details." Laurel leaned against the barn and tipped her head back, eyes closed, weary of the conversation.

Chance grinned. "Colt not a fan of the idea I take it." He hitched a boot on the bottom rail of the corral and leaned on the fence.

She cracked an eyelid and grimaced. "You could say that … and quit grinning."

He made a valiant effort, but the sides of his mouth kept twitching. "I really don't want you to go. You know how I feel about you, always have." He shrugged. "Can't help it."

Laurel opened her eyes and pushed away from the support of the barn. "I know, Chance. But I can't help wanting what I want either." She started to move toward the house. His hand on her arm halted her progress.

7

"I'm scared, Laurie."

Recognizing by the tightness of his voice how serious he was, Laurel refrained from kicking his ass for using her dad's pet name for her. Again. "Scared of what?" She turned to face him, the last bit of sunlight throwing his face into shadow.

"Of ... you know ... falling off the wagon." His grip on her arm tightened. "You going to the AA meetings with me when Carly can't means so much to me. I don't know how I'm gonna handle it if you're not here. Don't leave me, Laurie. Please."

"Don't beg, Chance. You've been doing so great, and you don't need me. It's not my responsibility to keep you on the straight and narrow, that's up to you. You know that ... and Dad and Mom are right here. Any time, day or night."

"But..."

"Chance Cullen, I'm not your security blanket. You can't hang that guilt on me if you slip up. That's on you." Laurel kept her voice stern even though her heart was breaking for her childhood friend. She cursed Cory Cullen to depths of the nine hells for what he'd done to his kids. She reached out and took Chance's hand. "C'mon in the house, Mom should have dinner ready, and you can give Dad the report on how things are going at the Diamond C." Laurel pulled him toward the house, laptop and papers tucked under her arm.

"Thanks, Laurel." He grinned at her surprised expression and slid his arm around her waist snugging her against his side. "Honestly, I don't know what I'll do without you around, but I promise I'll do my best." He dropped a kiss on the top of her head.

"Seriously, Cullen. Talk to Dad if you're feeling fragile. He's always had a soft spot for you. He's real proud of the way you're running the Diamond C, you and Carly."

"That's nice to hear."

The pair stopped at the foot of the broad steps up to the wide porch of the sprawling ranch house. He looked down at her and stepped away. "You do what you need to do. I'll be here waiting for you when you come home." Chance leapt up the steps and disappeared into the warmth of the house, leaving Laurel looking after him.

Shaking her head, she followed him, shedding her outdoor clothes in the hall.

"Laurel, come help your mom with dinner," Colt Rowan said, coming out of his office to walk toward the kitchen with his daughter.

"Sure, Dad. Where did Chance go? I asked him to stay for dinner." Laurel headed toward the sound of her mother singing.

"Washing up, I expect." Colt ruffled her hair. "Glad to see you two are getting along better these days."

She shrugged, shot him a quick smile, and entered the kitchen. "Hey Mom, what can I do?"

Anna Rowan looked up from the pot she was stirring. "Set the table, please. I see we have a guest for dinner."

"Hardly a guest. Chance is family." Colt crossed the floor to hug his wife and plant a kiss on the top of her head.

Anna shot a sharp glance at her daughter and winked. "Family in a way, I suppose," she agreed.

"Mom!" Laurel warned, not wanting to open up the subject of herself and Chance as a couple. Something she knew her father would be particularly happy about, should that ever come about.

"Thanks for having me for dinner." Chance strode into the room, his hair still showing wet comb marks.

"Anytime, son. You know you're always welcome at our table." Colt sat at the table and nodded at the chair beside him.

"'Preciate it." Chance parked his butt on the chair and leaned his elbows on the table.

"Long day?" Colt's gaze was steady on the younger man. "Trouble at the ranch?"

"No, sir. No trouble. Just a lot to get done..."

"Carly giving you grief again? You want me to talk to her?" Colt glanced at Laurel, who shook her head at him.

"Not really...well sort of...she's got poor Joey running in circles right now. Don't know what's got into her. I don't like the crowd she's runnin' with, but ya know... I'm just her bossy older brother." He rubbed a hand over his face.

Anna handed the pot of potatoes to Laurel and indicated she should drain them before coming to stand beside Chance. "I can talk to her if you want, she might listen to me where she won't to you."

"If you could, it might help. Mom isn't much help right now and Carly won't listen to her anyway."

"I'll see what I can do. Quit worrying, son. It'll all sort itself out, always does." Anna turned to take the platter of roast beef out of the warming oven and set it on the table.

"Here's the rest." Laurel plopped bowls of mashed potato and corn beside the meat.

Conversation lagged while they did justice to the food on the table.

Colt pushed his plate away and leaned back in his chair. "Thanks, Anna. Good as always." He got to his feet. "Come on in the den with me, Chance. Let's go over those numbers for last month again."

"Sure," Chance got to his feet and hesitated, "I should help with the dishes, least I can do after such a great meal."

"One you didn't have to cook yourself," Laurel teased him. "Go on, Mom and I've got this."

"The ladies have spoken." Colt laughed and slung an arm around the younger man's shoulder. "Let's leave them to it before they change their minds."

"You!" Anna threw a dish towel at her husband, laughing.

Chapter Two

"Everything looks good, Chance. I'd have to say the Diamond C is doing better than we expected." Colt leaned back in the big leather chair. "What's bothering you? Aside from Carly."

"Nothin'." Chance stared at a point somewhere over Colt's left shoulder.

"Let me guess, then. Laurie told you she wants to go back to Cornwall and it's eating at you."

Chance shrugged and took a deep breath. "Yeah. Why the hell does she want to do such a damn fool thing? She's got everything she could possibly want here."

"Everything?" Colt prodded.

"Sure." Chance met his gaze.

"Except for Coll and her friends, not to mention her grandmother," Colt's voice was soft.

"Yeah, except for that," bitterness edged Chance's voice.

"Son, you gotta give the girl room. The harder you push the more she'll resist. That's a hard lesson I learned when Anna and I were young."

"Mrs. Rowan gave you a hard time when you were dating?" Chance leaned forward.

Colt smothered a laugh that was more of a snort. "You could say that." He shook his head. "Trust me, you don't want to get a Rowan woman riled up."

"I've noticed." Chance grinned. "What do you think I should do? Just let Laurie head off to Cornwall and cross my fingers she'll come home?"

"Oh, she'll come home all right. I'm sure of that. Laurie's an Alberta girl at heart. I don't like the idea of her going over there again either. Getting mixed up in all that nonsense my mother is involved in … but she's got her heart set on it, and I guess maybe it's something she needs to get out of her system. If I were you, I'd back off and let her see you support her decision … even if you have to pretend."

"Yeah, I can't help how I feel about her leaving. If she decides to stay over there, I might never see her again and I don't know how to deal with that…"

"I told you, son. Laurie'll come home. You might just have to worry about whether she comes home alone?" Colt felt obliged to warn the young man across the desk from him about that possibility.

"You think I haven't thought about that too?" Chance ground his teeth.

"Well, keep it under your hat. Smile and wish her good luck. And you and I'll hope and pray she comes back soon and by herself. Now let's go see what the ladies are up to. I think we've wasted enough time to avoid drying any dishes." Colt pushed back from the desk, came around the desk, and slung an arm around Chance's shoulder as he stood up. "Cheer up. I know my girl. She'll come home safe and sound."

* * *

"What have you two been up to?" Anna quirked an eyebrow at her husband when the men returned to the kitchen. "Good timing as usual, we've just finished cleaning up. Ready for coffee?"

"You bet." Colt planted a kiss on his wife's forehead.

Laurel grinned and turned to the counter to pour coffee into four mugs.

"Here, let me help with that." Chance picked up two of the mugs and took them to the table.

"Thanks." Laurel smiled at him, relieved he seemed to be in a better mood than when Carly'd dropped the bomb about Laurel returning to Cornwall. She followed him to the table with the remaining mugs and set them by her parents. Settling into the chair beside Chance, she glanced sideways at him. "You still willing to help me out with the wild horse rescue paperwork and stuff?"

"Said I would, didn't I?" Chance downed a gulp of coffee.

"Good. I can count on you to keep things running while I'm away, right?"

Chance exchanged a covert glance with Colt over the rim of his mug. "Sure. Yeah. Just don't stay away too long."

"Thanks. No promises about how long I'll be gone though. If I get accepted there a bunch of hoops I need to jump through."

"You'll do fine, honey." Anna reached over and tousled her daughter's hair. "My little horse whisperer."

Laurel snorted. "Not hardly. I hate that term."

"Fair enough," Colt agreed. He picked up his mug and pushed back from the table. "Now I have some things I need to take care of." He kissed the top of Anna's head. "I'll be in the study. Chance, I think we covered everything we needed to earlier?"

"Yes, sir. I think so." He drained his coffee and stood up as well. "I need to get back to the Diamond C anyway. Got a few things need taking care of and I need to check on Carly."

"I'm sure Carly can take care of herself." Laurel smirked at him.

"That's what I'm worried about. Her and Joey are way too close for my peace of mind." Chance jammed his hat on his head.

"Carly's a big girl now. Don't go all big brother on her. You know how that goes," Laurel warned him.

He turned his attention to Laurel and took a step closer. "She tells you everything. If there's like something I should know about, you'd tell me, wouldn't you?" A small, worried frown creased his forehead.

Laurel leaned forward and put a hand on his arm. "You gotta trust her, Chance. It's her life and you can't protect her from making mistakes. I know for a fact, if I make a mistake, I want it to be my choice and not because I listened to someone else's advice."

"She's my little sister, a guy's got a right to worry." He shook his arm free. "Night, everyone. Thanks for dinner, Mrs. Rowan." His bootheels echoed down the hall before the door opened and closed.

Colt took the opportunity to escape to his paperwork. Anna regarded her daughter with a thoughtful expression.

"Are Carly and Joey getting really serious?" she ventured a question.

"Mom! What are you implying?" Laurel evaded a direct answer.

"You know what I'm asking," Anna persisted. "I love that girl like my own and I sure as hell don't want her to get into any trouble she can't get out of." She reached across the table and gripped Laurel's hand. "You either."

"Who am I going to get into trouble with?" Laurel joked. "Not Chance, and he's the only guy I see on a regular basis anymore."

"What about Coll? What about Cornwall? How strong are your feelings for him?"

"Honestly...I don't know. I haven't actually seen him in person in a long time and talking on social media and texting is great...but it's not the same. I mean, sometimes it feels like he has a life there I'm not part of and I have a life here he's not part of. But I don't want to give up the connection I have with Coll." She sighed and squeezed her mom's hand. "Why does it have to be so complicated."

"Oh, honey." Anna laughed. "Life is complicated. I don't know why, it just is."

"How do you know what to do, what to choose? What's the right decision or the wrong one?"

"That's like asking me what the meaning of life is, sweetie. All I can tell you is you have to follow your heart but listen to your common sense at the same time. Don't get carried away with your head in the clouds and your feet nowhere near the ground." Anna hesitated. "Are you sure you want to go to Cornwall? It could be for a couple of years if you get accepted. What can't you just keep teaching Pony Club here and stay involved with the 4H Horse Club?"

"I could. But Mom...I want more, and you know since I started competing in the combined training events and joined the Alberta Horse Trials Association how much I love the sport. I mean, I could go to Germany, they have an awesome program, but I'd have to learn to speak the language, which could be fun, but Cornwall is well...Cornwall."

"And Coll doesn't have anything to do with this sudden urge to go back to England?"

"A bit, he does. I want to see him and really talk with him. And I want to see Aisling and Gort. From what Ash tells me, they're pretty serious and now they're eighteen Aisling's mom can't very stand in their way anymore."

"Are you saying they're thinking of getting married?" Anna let go of Laurel's hand and sat back in her chair.

"I'm pretty sure they were just waiting for Ash to turn eighteen. Mom, I mean, they've been together since grade school, if not before. And Emily seems to be okay with the idea. Coll says she's trying to smooth things over between Ash and her mom. Did I tell you Ash is staying with Coll and his Gramma Emily now? In a separate room from Gort, though, if that's what that frown is about."

"Oh. I didn't know it had gotten that far. Well, I suppose they are considered adults." She fixed her daughter with a stern gaze. "You aren't thinking of anything like that with Coll, are you? That isn't what this whole working student thing is about, is it?"

"Mom!" Laurel stood up so fast her chair scooted backward. "No! Of course not. It's really about the horses and learning from the best. But, yeah, I want to see Coll and reconnect in person. But that doesn't mean I'm going to hop into bed with him or do something stupid. Besides, I want to see Gramma Bella while I'm there too, and Grampa Vear. Can't you understand that?"

"Alright, honey. Calm down. I had to ask. You'll understand when you're a mother and your little girl is all grown up and wanting to try her wings. Until then you'll just have to take my word for it, that your dad and I only want what's best for you."

"Sure, Mom. Sorry I got pissy, but honestly you need to trust me to make my own decisions. And make my own mistakes when I make them." She stepped around the table and hugged her mother. "I gotta go finish the budget for the wildies and make sure everything is in order for Chance when he takes over. Honest, I'll be fine. Love you." Laurel grinned and headed to her room.

"Love you too." Anna whispered as her daughter took the stairs two steps at a time.

Chapter Three

Laurel hovered the mouse, closed her eyes, and opened the email from Longrock Equestrian.

"Please, please, please," she whispered. "Please let it be good."

Her heart throbbing in her throat, she cracked open one eye. The morning sun shafted through the office window effectively fading the screen to near invisibility. Taking a deep breath, Laurel opened both eyes and shifted the laptop. The words on the screen blurred and ran together for a moment, their import refusing to register in her mind. She read the email another time, the information firing the synapses in her brain.

Dear Laurel,

We've received your application for the position of working student for the coming season. While your experience in the sport is somewhat limited, your coach's recommendation weighs heavily in your favour. We are pleased to welcome you to the Longrock Equestrian team and look forward to meeting you in person. Attached you will find the Working Student Agreement as well as more information on what will be expected of you and other practical considerations such as accommodation etc. Please complete and sign the agreement and return it to us as soon as possible. If for some reason you are unable to accept the position' please advise immediately as our waiting list is quite full.

Best Regards

Suzy Wish
BHS Stage 5 Performance Coach
(replaces BHSI)

She bolted to her feet, hand pressed to her chest to try and ease the thundering of her heart. "Oh my God, oh my God! I'm in, I'm going. Oh my God!"

Laurel crossed the office, and grabbing the handrail, fairly slid down the steps without touching them. She burst through the partly open door at the foot into the barn.

"Daddy..." Her voice was muffled by the solid chest she ran right into. "Oufff, Daddy, Daddy, guess what?"

Strong arms closed around her, holding her upright. Vibrating with excitement she looked, tears starting in her eyes. "Oh..." She tried to take a step back, but the arms held her tight.

"I'm not your dad, Laurie." Chance relaxed his hold a bit, but still kept his arms around her. "Good news, I take it? New wildie foals?" His lips smiled but it didn't reach his eyes.

"Better than that. Oh Chance, I got accepted! I got the working student position. I'm really going!" She pulled free of him, her boots echoing a happy dance down the barn aisle.

"Of course, you are," Chance muttered. "Of course, you are."

"Be happy for me, please?" Laurel came back to him and took his hands in hers. "I really want this. Really, really want this. Can't you be happy for me?"

Chance swallowed hard. "I am, Laurie. I know how hard you've worked and want to progress in the sport, I just don't understand why it can't be in Ontario or the States. There's tons of great stables right here in Canada."

She squeezed his hands. "I know that, but Cornwall is...Cornwall. I can't explain it...if you'd ever been there, felt what it's like...the cliffs, the ocean, the moors, riding on the beach with the sea coming in..."

"What's all the hollering about?" Colt Rowan came down the aisle from the tack stall. "I could hear you all the way outside. You two aren't feuding again, are you? Because I'm telling you both I'm sick to death of the nonsense..."

"It's nothing like that, Daddy." Laurel let the happiness and excitement explode out of her, shining in her eyes. "I got it, Daddy. I got accepted at Longrock!" She leaped into his arms.

Colt met Chance's gaze over her shoulder, one eyebrow cocked up in sympathy before he hugged his daughter and set her on her feet. "Congratulations, honey. I know this is what you want, even if I think it's not such a great idea." He held up his hand to stop her protest. "I said I'd support you in whatever you decided, and I will. Have you told your mom yet?"

"No, I just found out and came to find you, but I ran into Chance first, by accident."

"I got stuff to take care at the Diamond C, if you don't need me for anything else, Colt?" Chance stuffed his gloves in his back pocket and settled his hat more firmly on his head.

"You're good, son. Go take care of what needs doing. Call me later with your report on the south grain fields. They should dry enough on the high ground soon."

Chance nodded his agreement and disappeared out the end doors.

Laurel looked after him. "I wish he could be happy for me."

"He is, Laurie. It's just hard for him, you know that." Colt put an arm around her waist.

She sighed and frowned. "Why is it my problem that he thinks he's in love with me and I just like him as a friend?"

"No one is saying it's your problem or fault, it's just the way it is right now. Maybe he'll grow out of it in time." Colt soothed his daughter while doubting

Chance's love for her would ever get 'grown out of.' "Let's go tell your mom the good news."

Arm in arm the pair left the barn and headed to the house where the smell of coffee greeted them as they walked through the door.

"I'm going, Mom. I'm going to Cornwall. I got accepted." Laurel dashed into the kitchen and grabbed her mom to dance her around the room.

Laughing, Anna dropped into a chair while Colt poured three cups of coffee.

"I'm happy for you, sweetie. And proud, too." She glanced at her husband before returning her attention to Laurel. "Have you told Chance yet?"

"Yup, I went looking for Dad as soon as I got the email and ran right into Chance at the bottom of the stairs in the barn, so actually, he was the first to know."

Anna caught her daughter's chin in her hand and studied her face. "How did he take the news? I can't imagine he was overjoyed."

Laurel covered her mother's hand with her own and brought their joined hands to the table. "He was pretty good about it, really. Surprisingly enough because Carly repeats all his rants about me leaving and never coming back. She thinks it's amusing, to see him getting so worked up about what she thinks is nothing. I hate seeing him unhappy and I sure as hell don't want him to start drinking and using again."

"You can't let that stop you from following your dreams, honey." Anna stroked a hand over her hair.

"I'm not. Let me tell you. I love Chance, just not like he wants me to, but no way am I giving up my dreams to babysit him. He's older than I am, for God's sake. Chance Cullen is not my responsibility. No matter what Carly says," she muttered the last part.

"Is Carly putting pressure on you about her brother?" Anna leaned forward.

Laurel shrugged. "She's trying, but it's not going anywhere. I told her to worry about her own relationships and leave me alone about Chance."

"Good for you." Colt finished his coffee. "I need to run into Pincher for some supplies. Anybody need anything?" He unfolded his long frame and deposited his cup on the counter.

"I'm fine," Anna replied, lifting her face for his kiss.

"Not for me." Laurel jumped up. "I have to go text Coll and let him know." She glanced at the clock and frowned. "What time is it over there right now. Damn, I can never get it right."

"Bye." Colt's boots echoed down the hall followed by the door closing.

Anna laughed. "Whatever time it is, I'm sure he'll be glad to hear the news. Oh, look at that silly dog!" She pointed out the window to where Colt's pickup rolled by, Darby, the dog Laurel and Chance rescued from the dog fighting ring, with her head out the passenger window, tongue lolling, and joy on her face.

Laurel moved to the window to watch the pickup go up the lane. "For someone who put up such a fuss when I brought her home, Dad sure seems to like her a whole lot."

"That he does, but he'd never admit it." Anna smiled. "You know his bark is worse than his bite, the old softie."

"I wouldn't go that far." Laurel grinned, moving toward the door.

"Go on, go text Coll and make your plans." Anna waved her out the door.

Chapter Four

Laurel blinked the sleep from her eyes and leaned forward to peer out the plane window, eager to get a first glimpse of the English countryside. How green and lush it was compared to the Canadian prairie. Something unfolded in her chest while a glow of wellbeing and welcome swept over her.

"Hi, Gramma Bella," she whispered, feeling her grandmother's touch in the welcome. The flight attendants came through the cabin preparing for landing. Laurel tidied up her things that she'd somehow managed to spread around her on the long flight. Thank goodness Dad insisted she upgrade to first class with the nifty sleeping pod. At the time, she'd thought it was a bit extravagant but now Laurel was very glad he'd just gone ahead and booked it for her. With all her belongings stowed away, she settled back in the seat, attempting to tame the butterflies in her stomach. Her fingers touched the talisman on a leather thong around her neck. It was her link to Grampa Vear Du and Gramma Bella.

Will Coll have changed much since we were together? God, I'm nervous. I can't wait to see Ash and Gort and hear all about their plans. I wonder if they've managed to talk Ash's mom around yet?

Her thoughts were interrupted by the jolt of wheels hitting the runway and the roar of the big engines slowing the plane. She fiddled impatiently while the craft was made ready for deplaning, but finally, she followed the rest of the first class customers up the jetway into the waiting area. A quick glance showed her the way to the baggage claim and customs. The carousel was still immobile when Laurel arrived at the designated spot. She found a spot to sit and spent the time observing the people around her. It served to take her mind off Coll and helped steady her nerves.

Why am I so nervous? It's not like we haven't kept in touch and Face Timed almost every day. The thought of actually seeing him in person suddenly seemed like a way bigger deal than it should. The squeal of the baggage carousel coming to life brought her to her feet. *Please, please let my bag come down early.* Laurel stood by the baggage drop, eyeing each case that slid down the chute. Thankfully, her black bag with the red maple leaf on it came shooting out before too long. She hefted it off the moving surface and followed the signs to customs and the arrivals waiting area.

Customs was taken care of short order and before long Laurel was hurrying toward the sliding doors where the crowd of people waiting to greet friends and family gathered. The length of the long halls she needed to navigate was far longer than she remembered from her last visit. It seemed that Heathrow had undergone some renovations. There was a bewildering array of choices along the way, trains, the underground, surface transportation...Laurel began to worry she'd missed a turning when finally the hall spewed out into an open area. She scanned the sea of faces, searching for anyone who looked familiar. *Where are they?* She stopped and shifted her shoulder bag before moving forward.

"Laurel!" Strong arms engulfed her from behind. "I was starting to worry you'd missed your plane." Coll hugged her and then turned her to face him. "It's so good to see you."

"Coll!" She hugged him back and looked up at him. "I can't believe I'm actually here. Where are Ash and Gort?"

"They're waiting for us at Sairie's." He grinned. "They thought we might like some time alone together. C'mon, the Heathrow Express train is this way. We've got first class tickets for the train from Paddington to Penzance, Sairie's doing." Coll glanced at the time on his phone. "We've got scads of time, but we should go, it's a fair way to the platform and it's most likely crowded with all the flights getting in so close to each other."

"Sounds like a plan. Let's go." She stepped away from him but let him keep her hand in his. Coll pushed her suitcase along beside them. "I don't remember it being quite this crazy," she remarked while they threaded their way through the crowd.

"I don't get up to London much, but yeah, it does seem a bit nuts, doesn't it?"

* * *

They found seats on the Express and in fifteen minutes they stepped off in Paddington station. The glass roof arched high above them. Laurel had to stop herself from staring up at it. For some reason the domed roofs of the London train stations fascinated her. After tripping over someone's foot and then bumping into a grumpy businessman, she kept her eyes forward and let Coll lead her toward the platform where the Great Western Railway train waited. The station bustled with commuters disgorging from other trains, emerging from the underground, and entering from the street on both sides of the station. The rumble of noise vibrated through her feet, and she gripped Coll's hand tightly.

She shook her head at the silliness. It was just people and noise, not to mention she'd been to London and taken this train before. Still, it was so far divorced from the openness of the Alberta prairie and the noises she was used to that it was a bit overwhelming.

"Thanks for meeting me," she half-shouted to Coll. "This place is way crazier than I remember."

He grinned over his shoulder. "Ash and Gort wanted to come too like I said, but I talked them out of it. I want you all to myself for a while." He stopped by a first-class car and pressed the button to activate the doors. "Here we are, let's stow your bag and get a seat. With any luck it won't be busy today and we'll not have to share with anyone."

Laurel stepped into the car and waited while Coll stowed her suitcase in the cubby by the door. He caught her hand again and headed down the car to a set of seats with two facing forward and two facing backward. They took the forward-facing seats, Laurel set her backpack on the floor by her feet and leaned an elbow on the small table between the two sets of seats.

"I can't wait to see everyone. It feels like forever since we were all together."

"Feels like it to me too. I missed you a lot, Laurel." He paused. "How are things with Chance? Is he still being a tosser?"

She shook her head. "Actually, he's been acting almost like a human lately. He's looking after the wildies while I'm gone. Doing all the paperwork and checking that everything is good with them."

Coll sniffed and shifted in his seat. "That's good then, I guess. Does he still fancy himself in love with you?"

"Maybe...I guess...honestly, it's not something I ever talk to him about. The less said the better as far as I'm concerned."

"Your dad still in Chance's corner?"

"I wouldn't say that exactly." It was Laurel's turn to pause and choose her words. "Dad is pretty close with him, but I think that's because he feels responsible. I mean Chance doesn't have anyone he can depend on except my parents. And now that Dad's bought the Diamond C, well, he has to work closely with him."

"Yeh, I can see where that would complicate matters." Coll twined his fingers with hers as the train started to move. "Penzance, here we come."

Laurel leaned back in the seat and rested her head against the window, watching the soot blackened brick walls slide by, then the terrace houses and other buildings as the train picked up speed. Before too long, they passed the outskirts of London and entered the much more soothing English countryside. She looked up when Coll got to his feet.

"Do you want anything? I'm going to the see if there's a buffet car on this train or if we have to order off the app."

"Some kind of sandwich and something to drink would be great. Things have changed if there's an app for ordering food on the train now." She laughed.

"I downloaded it at home just in case. It depends on the train right now which way it goes. Sarie made sure you'd be well taken care of." He headed off down the swaying car.

Laurel leaned forward to get a better look at the White Horse carved into the chalk hillside shining in the sun. One day, she promised herself, she was going to visit one of the many chalk figures. Hopefully the White Horse of Uffington in Wiltshire, which was her personal favourite. But really, any of them would do, she supposed. There was something so otherworldly and magical about them. The Cerne Giant would be interesting, for sure. She grinned.

Thinking of horses, she dragged her backpack up onto her lap and pulled out the information from Longrock Equestrian. Even though she'd read the information at least a hundred times, her stomach still curled with excitement at the thought of riding unknown horses and being faced with bigger and wider obstacles than she'd jumped at home.

"Ordered from the app. It should be along soon." Coll slid back into the seat beside her. "Is that all the stuff about Longrock?"

"Yeah. It's kind of overwhelming now it's actually happening," she admitted.

"I bet your mom and dad wish you'd just taken the Canadian programs you were telling me about."

"For sure. But this is way better and I'll get to travel to all the big events with Suzy and everyone. With all that experience I should be able to generate enough income to keep myself and the wildies cared for. Gramma Bella's inheritance is invested, and I still have the property in Bragg Creek, but with the stock market the way it is and the craziness in the world right now, I want to make sure there's a back up plan. Besides, I wanted to come back to Cornwall and see everything again and maybe see if I can visit Gramma Bell and Vear Du." She fished the old talisman out of the front pocket of her jeans.

"Do you think it still works?" Coll touched it with a finger. "I mean, it's been a fair long time."

"I know. I hope it still works. I was thinking of maybe trying it at Carn les Boels and Boscawen'en Stone Circle. I figure if it will work anywhere, those might be the two best places."

"What about Nanjizal? It worked there before," Coll reminded her.

"Yes, of course. How could I have forgotten that? Nanjizal might be just the place and not too hard to get to either. Coll, you're a genius." She leaned over and kissed him. "The Song of the Sea," she whispered, referring to the slit in the cliff that flooded at high tide and had served as a portal for Gramma Bella in the past.

He kissed her back with his arm around her shoulder. "The Song of the Sea," he repeated, supressing a shudder. The whole magics thing still bothered him, it felt like a buzz on his skin.

Laurel kept her gaze on the passing scenery, drinking in the height of the trees, nearly even with her window as the train swept over the high trestles before dropping down to skirt the edge of the English Channel as the track turned at Dawlish just before crossing the River Tamar and coming into Plymouth. It was all she could do to keep her eyes open as the long flight and the lulling motion of the train threatened to overcome her. The sight of the "Welcome to Kernow" sign sent a thrill of excitement through her.

"Almost there." She squeezed Coll's hand.

"Almost home," he said. "They'll most likely be waiting at the station."

"Who?" Laurel half turned in her seat. "Ash and Gort? I'm starving, even after the lunch you bought. We can go to that old pub with the smugglers well in the courtyard."

"The Admiral Benbow, you mean. There'll be more than Ash and Gort, I think. Pretty sure Gramma and Sairie will be there for sure, maybe Stuart..."

"Stuart?" Her voice rose in surprise. "Are you guys buds now? After he was such an asshat when you were in school? Him and his gang."

"He's not such a git now. We actually get along pretty well when we see each other, which isn't all that often."

"Then why would he be there?" Laurel was truly puzzled.

Coll shrugged. "He was tending bar at the Turk's Head when Gort and I were having a pint a couple of weeks ago. You'd just texted to say you were coming for sure and I was telling G about it. Stuart overheard and he remembered you and said we should be sure to come in for a meal or something. That he'd like to see you again."

"And you think he'll show up at the train station?"

"Maybe. I don't know Laurel. What chance does a bloke have when you've got men hanging off your every word wherever you go?" Coll grinned, but there was an underlying vulnerability under the words.

Laurel cuffed him on the arm. "Get out! Besides, it doesn't matter what guys think, it's who I want to hang with that counts. And that's you, and Ash and Gort. Wait. Did you call him G?"

"Yeah. It just kinda happened. Ya know, Gort...G. It's quicker and easier. Ash started it and it just caught on. Course, Gramma and Sairie don't call him that."

"Hmmmm, something I'll have to get used to, I guess." She looked up as the train pulled into yet another station. "Hayle. That's fairly close, isn't it? I can't remember for sure, but I think I remember we went there to visit Hamish, the famous dowser. Or am I wrong?"

"Nope, you're right on. Almost home. Yeah. Remember how we walked up to that old hill fort and then went exploring along the estuary when the tide was out. That was a fun day."

"It was. I love watching the tide go in and out, little bit by little bit sliding up and down the sand until suddenly the water's up to your ankles or slipping way out toward the sea. I miss that at home." She looked at the sea, bright blue in the sun and ruffled by the wind.

"We'll make a point of going for a picnic on one of your days off."

"That would be awesome." She snuggled into the seat and rested her head on the backrest. "I can't wait to get there, but then I wish this trip could go on forever, just you and me and Cornwall."

"The train ride can't last forever, but you and me and Cornwall, that could be forever, if you wanted." Coll took her hand, the atmosphere suddenly serious.

"Whoa, where did that come from all of a sudden?" Heat stole up Laurel's neck. The shift from happy and relaxed to totally something else set her on edge.

"I think you know how I feel about you, always have. Right from the start when we were solving that riddle so we could help your mom. It killed me when you left the last time."

"We've kept in touch, though. And you came to visit the ranch." She laid a hand on his arm.

"Yeah. It's not enough, Laurel. This long-distance relationship thing is hard. I want you here, with me, to share everything. Go to dances, and parties, ride Sairie's ponies across the moor. We're not kids anymore."

"No, you're right. We're not kids anymore, but...wow...just wow. I have responsibilities at home, the wildies, helping Dad with the ranch. I even have some students that I coach at a beginner level right now. I can't just pull up stakes..."

"Will you think about it...what I've said. Promise me you'll think about it." Coll pulled her close and crushed his mouth to hers. "Promise," he said after pulling back.

Laurel gazed at him, unsure how to respond to the urgency in his voice and body. The train lurched to a stop at Penzance, saving her from an immediate answer. "Later. We'll talk about it later. Right now, we're here! Look, there's Ash and Gort!" Laurel gathered her backpack and urged Coll to get up and head to the exit. She snagged her suitcase from the cubby while Coll pressed the button and the door hissed open.

"Ash!" Laurel all but tumbled off the train step onto the platform, tripping over her bag and dropping her backpack. She threw herself into her friend's arms, hugging her tight, laughing and crying at the same time. "Look at you! You look great." She caught Ash's hand as they stepped back. "What's this?" Laurel turned Ashling's left hand to catch the light. "The rumours are true? I'm so happy for you." She hugged her again.

"Hey, what about me?" Gort stood by grinning, watching the two young women greet each other. "No hug for me?"

"Of course." She turned to him, sliding her arms around him. "You've gotten taller since I saw you last, and broader in the shoulders, for sure. You been working out or something?" Laurel stepped back and grinned. "Congratulations, you two. I'm so happy for you."

"Me too," Gort said, taking Aisling's hand. "Now you're finally here we can start planning."

"Planning?" Laurel stared at her two friends. "Are you kidding me?"

Ash shook her head. "We've been hoping my mum would come around to accepting this, but she hasn't, and I don't think she will. So we decided not to wait, but to set a date."

"Then Coll told us you were coming to do some horsey thing and we thought, well, there now. Let's have the ceremony when Laurel is here too." Gort took up the narrative.

"Here now, let an old lady through." Sairie elbowed the couple aside laughing. "Come give me a hug, you." She enfolded Laurel against her ample bosom.

"Sairie, Sairie. I've missed you so much. I wish you would come and visit, but here I am now. So let's not waste any time."

"I missed you too." She held Laurel at arm's length. "Look at you, you're all grown up. Even since those graduation pictures you sent. A young lady you are now."

"If you say so." Laurel laughed. "Dad might disagree with you on the lady part."

"Come along then. Let's get you home and settled for now. Coll, get her bag please." Sairie hustled Laurel toward her little car.

"We can all fit in that?" Laurel exclaimed.

"Not to worry. Our Coll has his own auto now, so no one will have to walk to the farm."

"Good, then." Laurel caught Coll's hand as he put the suitcase in the boot. "You're coming with me, right?"

"If there's room. Alright if G takes my car?" He glanced at Sairie and Gramma Emily.

Emily nodded and the other three moved off toward the smart little red car beside Sairie's older, beat up faded blue one.

"Of course there's room. Emily can have shot gun and you and I can squeeze in the back."

"Shot gun?" Emily giggled. "We're not in your wild west now, girl."

"You know what I meant." Laurel patted her arm and slipped into the back seat, scrunching over so Coll could join her. Once they were in and Emily ensconced in the front, she twined her fingers with his and leaned her head on his shoulder. "It's nice to be back."

"It could be home." Coll nuzzled his face in her hair.

Laurel decided to pretend she hadn't heard. Her brain was muzzy with jet lag and Coll's sudden serious turn was perplexing. Nothing in their online conversations had even touched on moving their relationship to another level. Maybe, she mused, it was because of Gort and Aisling planning their wedding that had Coll thinking about something more permanent. *Do I want to move to Cornwall for good, leave the ranch and everything? Dad would go bat shit crazy if I even mentioned the idea. Mom would be more understanding, but I can't imagine she'd be thrilled either. And I don't even want to think about what Chance would say.*

Laurel straightened up and put a little space between her and Coll. The car careened along the narrow road, flowering hawthorn brushing the sides of the vehicle.

"I'd forgotten how narrow the roads are. And how fast you drive, Sairie."

"Now, now. I don't go any faster than what's necessary to get from one place to another." She took a sharp turn at speed.

"Uh huh," Laurel muttered. "And Dad thinks I drive like a maniac."

Coll glanced out the rear windscreen. "Gort's behind us, but back quite a way. He better not scratch my paint."

"How is he supposed to avoid that? With the hedge practically growing in the road." Laurel shook her head and grabbed the side of the front seat as Sairie stepped on the accelerator and forced an oncoming motorist to zip into a layby.

"It can be done," Coll insisted.

Laurel let a silent sigh of relief pass her lips when Sairie turned into the long lane of the farm. The barn with the black Fell ponies at the gate and the stone house looked exactly as she remembered them. Déjà vu swept over her. For a moment it felt like just yesterday she'd come up the lane for the first time. Maybe time wasn't linear, but folded back on itself so you could step from one time to another. Sairie, braking hard by the garage, interrupted her thoughts.

"Here we are now. Out with you. Coll, you take that suitcase up to Laurel's old room." Sairie stepped out and with her hands on her hips, arched her back. " I swear, some days I feel every one of my years."

Laurel hugged her. "No way. You're ageless, that's what you are."

"Pack horse, that's what I am," Coll joked as he hauled the suitcase out of the boot and headed for the house.

Laurel went to the gate where the Fell Ponies were waiting. She pushed aside the heavy black forelock to rub the white star on the nearest one.

"Ebony, look at you. You don't look a day older than the last time I saw you." She planted a kiss on the pony's nose.

"Here you are, Lamorna." She slipped through the bars of the gate to run her hands over the larger black mare. Laurel tipped her head toward Sairie. "She's aging well. How old is she now...fifteen or sixteen?"

"Aye, my Morna girl is seventeen in the summer this year. Hardly seems possible it's been that long since I brought a long-legged little filly home."

"How old was she when you got her?" Laurel scratched along the hairline under the thick mane. The mare leaned into the pressure, eyes closing in contentment.

"A yearling, she was. And a bright little thing, I never expected her to get so large. But there you have it." Sairie smiled. "I'd not change a thing about her."

The crunch of tires on gravel announced Gort's arrival. He parked the little red car before he, Ashling, and Emily joined Sairie at the gate.

"I might have known you'd be visiting the horses before going inside," Ash teased.

"What else would I do?" Laurel teased back. She glanced toward the car. "Where's Stuart? Didn't he come too?" With a final pat to Lamorna, Laurel greeted the two geldings, Arthur, and Gareth.

"Stuart asked us to drop him in Marazion. Said he didn't want to intrude and was happy he got to say hello to you when you arrived."

"That's silly. He could have come and be welcome," Laurel said. "You guys are all friends now, right?"

Gort shrugged. "Mostly. He's still Stuart, if you catch my meaning, even though he's really working on being a better bloke. That father of his, though..."

Laurel slipped back through the gate and linked arms with Ashling. "Is his dad, what was his name...Ted? Anyway, is he still the head of police here? His mom was Angela, right?"

"Yeah, the bloody git is still Chief Constable," Coll said, rejoining them. "What did you pack in that suitcase? It weighs a ton."

"Coll!" Emily chided him. "Let the girl alone, she probably has all her riding gear in there."

"Just stuff." Laurel shrugged. "And yeah, my boots and show clothes along with my regular things. I had to leave my saddle at home."

"Come along, let's go wet the tea and catch up." Sairie herded the group toward the back door.

Coll caught Laurel's hand as the followed Ash and Gort behind Sairie and Emily.

"Hey, Sairie. Where are Morgen and Vivienne? I don't see them in the field?"

"Well now, didn't I lend them out to group doing plowing demonstrations for a month or so. They'll be well taken care of as I visit them a couple of times a week."

"That sounds cool, can we go and see a demonstration sometime?"

"That, my love, depends on your schedule. You're a working girl now, remember?"

"Oh crap, yeah, that reminds me." Laurel pulled out her phone and texted Suzy that she'd arrived and was getting settled in.

The rest of the afternoon was spent around the kitchen table, involving many pots of tea along with scones and biscuits. Finally, Emily announced it was time to be getting home. Gort and Ashling took their dishes to the sideboard and hauled Coll out of his chair. His reluctance to leave was obvious to Laurel, but in a small way she really wanted to be alone with Sairie, and with herself. Now that she was actually here, her nerves were starting to pick up. *What if I'm not good enough for Suzy's yard? What if the horses are bigger and stronger than what I'm used to jumpin?. And the fences! Those cross-country fences looked awesome in the photos on the website, but now the reality of actually pointing a horse at them and going for it...God, it makes me want to hurl. Stop it.* Laurel smothered her internal critic. *You were good enough to get the working student spot, Suzy must have been happy with what she saw on the videos we sent. Think of all I can learn here, and won't it be awesome to send some pics home of me over some of those jumps.* The image of the big table jumps flickered through her

35

mind, along with the fence at the top of steep drop. *Okay, maybe not those particular jumps just yet.*

"Laurel." Sairie waved her hand in front of her face. "Earth to Laurel. Are you okay, my love? You've gone all still and your face is pale."

"No, no. I'm fine. Just thinking about starting work the day after tomorrow. I'm excited and scared all at the same time," she confessed.

Sairie laughed and put her arm around her. "That's only natural, my gold. I'd be more inclined to worry about you if you weren't nervous."

Laurel got up from the chair, and Sairie rose along with her. She hugged the older woman before releasing her to take her dishes to the sideboard. When she made to start the washing up, Sairie stopped her with a hand on her arm.

"Here now, let me take care of that. Tomorrow is soon enough for you to start helping out around here. Take yourself upstairs for a nap or have a read in the front room if you like. Those three friends of yours are always leaving the new bestsellers laying around when they're finished with them." Sairie shook her head. "Some of the nonsense you young people read these days. Go on, scat. Out of my kitchen." Sairie softened the command with a kiss on Laurel's cheek.

"I've missed you so much." Laurel squeezed her hand. "Have you seen Gramma Bella and Vear at all? Since I left last time, I mean?"

Sairie leaned back on the counter for a moment, eyes faraway. "The last time I saw that pair was Alban Arthuan, winter solstice," she clarified in case Laurel had forgotten the old term. "I went to Boscawen'en to watch the sunset on the longest night and then to see the new sun rise on the first day of strengthening light."

"Gramma Bella and Vear were there with you?" Laurel fingered the talisman in her pocket.

"Didn't they show up just as the sun was tipping over the horizon. Vear stepped out of the leaning centre

36

stone and Bella from the white quartz stone in the north-east. I have to say it was wonderful to see them."

"How did they look? Are they okay?" Laurel clenched her hand in her pocket.

Sairie laughed. "Better than me, I must say. Bella hasn't aged a day since I last saw her, and well, your grandfather, he is as handsome as ever. And just as charming. They asked after you, of course, although they seem to be able to keep an eye on you from a distance, as they already were aware of your horse rescue and your involvement with those men who were hurting the dogs." Sairie paused and her expression became serious. "Vear wanted me to warn you off that young man. Chance, is it? He worries about you, does your grandfather."

"Chance is okay, Sairie. Really. He's had a rough go, and he's really trying to turn things around. Dad is supporting him and trying to step in and be the father Chance never had. It's easier now that Mister Cullen is dead, and his mom is in therapy. Although, Mrs. Cullen doesn't seem to want much to do with him, she's more interested in Carly. It's hard for him."

Sairie held up her hands. "You don't need to defend your friend to me, my love." She grinned. "Bella took Vear to task for even mentioning such a thing. Reminded him of how everyone thought her getting involved with him was such a bad idea and how horribly that turned out when her da shipped her off to Canada to marry some man she didn't even know. Thanks be to God that D'Arcy Rowan was a good open-minded man."

"Maybe I can see them while I'm here." Laurel closed her eyes and wished.

"Maybe you will. Maybe you will. Now run along and let me get the kitchen put to rights."

"I think I'm going to take a walk and maybe visit with the ponies for a bit." Laurel headed for the door.

"Off you go, then." Sairie flipped the dishcloth at her departing back.

Chapter Five

Slanting rays of the setting sun gilded the grass and hedgerow with gold. Laurel inhaled deeply and threw her head back letting the rich scent of earth, horse, lush pasture, and the faint salt of the water in Mount's Bay wash over her. Smiling, she slipped through the gate and spent a few moments fussing with the Fell ponies. She straightened Ebony's thick wavy forelock so it lay neatly between her eyes, almost obscuring the large white star on her broad forehead. Giving the mare one last caress, Laurel set off across the wide field, following the hedgerow where hawthorn and brambles bloomed snowlike peeking from within the bower of greenery. The odd flash of pink and purple of the early fuchsia blooms caught her attention as she wandered along. Her path took her toward the small valley that cut through the end of the property. It was here, five years ago, she'd run to cry her eyes out about being shipped off to Cornwall while her mom was so sick. A tiny part of her still hadn't forgiven her dad for that, but in the end, it all turned out for the best. Mom regained her health and Laurel made three life-long friends, along with Sairie and Emily.

Laurel shook her hair free of the tiny branches that reached out to her as she descended the narrow path down into the valley. Nothing had changed that she could see, the green light of the vale filtered through the canopy overhead and the musical voice of the, as yet unseen, tiny rill filled the air. Birds sang and twittered, filling the air with song, seemingly undisturbed by her presence. She paused for a long moment to let the peace and serenity of the place seep into her. A zephyr of warm air tingled over her skin, brushing her tangled hair from her face. Embracing the loveliness of the place she moved on. If memory served her correctly, the rill cascading down the shoulder of the vale should be just ahead on her right. Stepping through a shaft of sunlight, she stopped and caught her breath. There it was. Just as she remembered. She scrambled up the side of the waterway until she entered the small dell where the water pooled into a circular well. Water ribboned down the side of the hill from above her and paused in the pool before cascading the rest of the way to the valley floor.

Sitting on a convenient flat boulder by the edge of the pool. Laurel trailed her hand in the water. Tiny white and purple violets bloomed in profusion in the dark fertile soil, their delicate scent perfuming the air. Fern waved their fronds in the tiny breeze created by the falling water. The movement was mesmerizing as they danced, lifted, fell, and brushed against each other. *One day I'm going to bring Mom here. She'll love this place, the magic and the quiet.* Laurel closed her eyes for a moment, soaking in the atmosphere. As she opened them three small leaves twirled and twisted in the green tinted air while they spiraled toward the clear water of the pool. Her gaze followed their path until they settled on the still surface. Tiny ripples radiated out from each one until they butted up against each other, cancelling out the movement.

A sudden spear of sunlight blinded Laurel for a second. *How can that be? The sun must be almost down by now.* She blinked hard a few times to clear the bright spots from her vision. A woman swam into view through her watering eyes. The woman's blue eyes were smiling, and her skin glowed with an inner light. Her bright silvery blond hair lay in waves of spun cobweb over the blue robe on her shoulders. Laurel's

39

breath caught in her throat, and she reached out a hand to touch the woman as she sank down beside her.

"Lady? Is it really you?" Her words came out on a breath of whisper.

The White Lady's laugh mingled with the tinkle of the stream. "And who else would it be, sweet girl?" She smoothed a hand over Laurel's hair. "Look how grown up you are. No girl now, but a woman grown. Ready to take those first magic steps into womanhood." She smiled. "Maiden, Mother, Crone. In our time, we are all things in their turn and all things at once."

"I thought I'd never see you again." Laurel threw her arms around the radiant spirit. "Thank you so much for helping me when Mom was sick. I remember you every night when I say my prayers."

"I remember you as well, dear one. Such spirit and such courage. While I could not follow you or assist you in your quest, I did follow your journey. I sometimes see your gramma on the other side of the Veil where she chooses to live with her selkie husband."

Laurel released the Lady and clapped her hands. "Oh! They got married?"

The Lady laughed again. "They were always married, dear one. Theirs is a marriage of the spirit and the heart. They are married in love. Nothing else matters but the love."

"I suppose you're right," Laurel agreed.

"And what of you?" She tilted Laurel's face up toward her. "I see two paths open to you, but I see you are conflicted and unsure which one is the one you should take."

Laurel shrugged one shoulder. "I just want to do what's right, for everyone."

"You must do what is right for you. Remember, there really is no right or wrong, only a choice of which path you wish to take and how to live your life."

"But how do I know which one? I don't know. I just don't know. I love Coll, and I'm really connected to Chance, I mean I've known him since we were kids and of course I love him too. How am I supposed to decide?"

"That is up to you, sweet girl. In the end, you must follow your heart."

"What if my heart doesn't know? It sure feels like that right now." Laurel shook her hair out of her face, tucking a strand behind her ear.

The Lady smiled, tiny diamonds of light shining in her hair, haloing around her. "When the time is come, you will know. Your indecision just means the time is not yet come."

"But how will I know?" Laurel persisted.

"You will know. Trust me and trust yourself." In a graceful movement the Lady rose and held out a hand to Laurel. "It is time I was moving on, and time for you to return to the cottage. Sairie is beginning to be worried about you."

Laurel took the outstretched hand and got to her feet.

"How do you know Sairie's worried about me?"

"Why I can hear her, of course."

"What?" Laurel shook her head.

With a sigh the Lady tipped her head to regard Laurel with a penetrating stare. "So many questions." A frown marred her beautiful face for a second. "Sairie is connected to this land, she is its guardian, its steward. I am part of the land, I am the White Lady of the Spring, this spring, and others in this part of Kernow. Because of this mutual connection I can sense her emotions, sometimes her thoughts, if she is thinking very loud."

"Wow. Does she know this? Can she hear you?"

"Sairie is what Sairie is, so of course she is aware of the connection. How well she can sense me, or *hear* me if you like, depends on how open her heart is at any given time."

"Huh." Laurel was at a loss for anything else to say.

"Now, I must go. The sun has gone to bed and the moon is rising. Time for you to return to Sairie and time for me to get on with my duties." She kissed Laurel's brow and stepped back. "It is good to visit with you again, dear one. Blessed Be."

A shower of sparks and spiralling leaves blinded Laurel for a split second, and when she could see again, the Lady was gone, but her voice lingered in the air.

"Go gently," Laurel said before turning her feet toward home. When she topped the edge of the valley, she was surprised to see how much time had passed. The light was almost gone from the sky, the first stars pinpricking the delicate blue velvet of the coming night and the moon a shining sliver that would soon wax and fatten into the first quarter.

"A new moon, a new beginning," Laurel whispered and was sure she heard the Lady's voice echoing her words. Grinning, Laurel threw her head back and ran through the meadow, drinking the magic of the night. She slowed as she drew near the ponies gathered by the gate. Sairie was retrieving the feed buckets the ponies had just finished emptying.

"Sairie!" she called. "Sorry I was gone so long." Laurel picked up the last two buckets and handed them over the gate before coming through herself.

"Meeting with an old friend?" Sairie tilted her head with a knowing look in her eyes.

"You could say that," Laurel agreed.

"All is well, then?" Sairie put an arm around Laurel's shoulders as they made their way to the cottage.

"It is. Better than well, I think."

"Well then, lets get some supper in you and then bed. You have a big day tomorrow."

"Yeah. I don't officially start until the day after, but I have to go meet with Suzy, sign some papers, and get to see the horses and the set up." She danced a few steps. "I'm so excited I could just burst."

"Now don't be doing that, my love. T'would be more than a bit messy. Exploding and all."

Laughing the two women set the grain buckets in the mud room and went to make supper.

Chapter Six

The sky was still clothed in the last vestiges of night while the sleepy twitter of birds heralded the faint pre-dawn glow glimmering behind the trees when Laurel threw back the covers and padded to the window. Mist swirled over the pasture, wreathing the dark ponies so they appeared to float or swim over the grass rather than walk. Laurel listened for sounds from down the hall. Sairie must still be in bed. She picked up her phone to check the time. It was early, but Laurel was too keyed up to try and go back to bed.

Today was the day. Not her first official day of work, but everything she'd dreamed of, imagined a hundred times, was about to become reality. In just a few hours, Sairie was going to drop her off at Longrock and she'd get to meet Suzy in person and the horses. A frown wrinkled her face. Coll kept offering to drive her to the stable yard and wait for her. She sighed. *Why can't he back off a bit? Give me some room to think. I don't want to feel pressured for time because he's sitting there waiting for me.* Laurel pushed the thoughts away and concentrated on what she would need to take with her this morning. Not much really. She planned to wear her riding clothes and the custom made boots she'd saved money for forever to buy. Dad offered to buy her new riding boots but drew the line at the cost of the custom ones. She grinned at the memory of him teasing her about the tomfoolery (his words) of spending that much money on boots that were invariably going to get wet and dirty. Laurel glanced at the gleaming leather of the boots sitting by the dresser, upright in their boot holders. *As if mud or muck will stay on those babies for long.*

The hall floorboards creaked under Sairie's feet as she passed the door. Laurel pulled it open and giggled at Sairie's startled expression.

"Up already, are ye?"

"Couldn't sleep any longer. Let me get dressed and I'll come help with the chores and breakfast."

As if in answer to her words, nickers from the ponies gathered at the gate came through the open window. The rooster raised his voice from the chicken house.

"I swear they can read my mind." Sairie laughed.

"Maybe they can." Laurel giggled. "I'll be down in a sec." She ducked back into her room and dressed in jeans and a shirt. Time enough after chores and breakfast to change into her riding clothes.

* * *

Chores and breakfast taken care of, Laurel hurried upstairs to change. She listened with trepidation for the crunch of tires on gravel. It would be just like Coll to ignore her request and show up, insisting on driving her. Instead of pulling on the tall boots, she opted for her Ariats and slid the shining boots into the boot bag. If she got to ride today it would be easy to change into them, but she didn't want to appear presumptuous. Dad's words echoed in her ear: You only get one shot at a good first impression.

Slinging the boot bag onto her arm, she grabbed a light jacket and pulled it on over the cotton short sleeve T-shirt tucked into her breeches. *Time to go, it's time.* She danced to the door, resisting the urge to sing out loud. Bounding down the stairs two at a time, she skipped down the hall and into the kitchen.

"Look at you. All ready to go off and make a name for yourself." Sairie enfolded her in a hug. "You be

45

careful, you hear. I had me a look at some of them big fences. No way I want to have to call your mom and dad and tell them you've come a cropper."

Laurel hugged her back and stepped away. "I promise I'll be careful. I doubt very much that Suzy will let me anywhere anything challenging until she sees how well I ride."

"Still. Be careful."

"I will. Cross my heart."

"Let's get you there then." Sairie hustled her out the door.

No sign of Coll. Laurel heaved a silent sigh of relief. It wasn't that she didn't want to share this experience with him, it was just something she needed to do on her own without worrying about someone waiting for her to finish. She hopped in the front seat with Sairie and attempted to corral the butterflies in her stomach.

The drive to Longrock Equestrian from Sairie's cottage wasn't far. She turned to the driver as they sped along far too fast for Laurel's comfort.

"You know, if I got a bike I could ride to work and back. That would save you having to drive me and if I worked late or something I wouldn't have to worry about inconveniencing anyone."

Sairie glanced at her. "I think we can arrange that. I believe there's a bike in the shed you can use. I'll pull it out when I get home and see what needs seeing to. One thing though. There will be no riding bikes in the dark. Far too dangerous. Understood?"

"Sure." Laurel shrugged, one eye on the tall row of bushes brushing against the car. Riding alone in the dark with the branches reaching out to snag at her wasn't high on her list of things she wanted to do, for sure.

"Here we are, then." Sairie turned into the drive of Longrock Equestrian. "I'll just drop you off by the office and make myself scarce." She braked and squeezed Laurel's arm. "Luck. Call me when you're ready to come home."

"Thanks for the ride. I don't know how long I'll be today, but starting tomorrow I should have a better idea of a schedule." Laurel gathered her boot bag and stepped out of the car. Before entering the office, she waited while the blue Volkswagen whipped around and sped down the lane. Shaking her head and grinning, Laurel tapped on the door before going in.

"Hullo, can I help you?" The young blond woman at the desk looked up.

"Hi...I'm Laurel Rowan. I have an appointment with Suzy Wish. Ummm. I'm the new working student." Laurel hesitated in the doorway, her heart in her throat. *Do I have the wrong place?*

A smile broke across the woman's face. "Well, of course you are. I'm Miriam, welcome to Longrock. Suzy's around here somewhere. I'll text her and let her know you've arrived." She waved a hand toward a couple of seats by the window.

Laurel nodded her thanks but stayed standing. Her fingers twisted the strap on her boot bag until she forced herself to stop. The door on the far side of the room burst open, Laurel stifled her urge to jump.

"Laurel, welcome. Sorry I wasn't here to welcome you." Suzy Wish crossed the small space to shake Laurel's hand. Energy crackled around her.

"Thanks," Laurel almost stammered. *Holy cow, she's like lightning in a bottle.*

"Come along, I'll show the layout. You can leave your boots here, the stables are this way." Without waiting to see if Laurel was following, Suzy sailed out the door.

Laurel tucked her boot bag beside a chair and caught up with her. The stables were open and airy. Stalls lined both sides of a wide aisle. Stall guards allowed the horses to stand with their head out into the aisle and open doors at both ends ensured there was plenty of air movement. A couple of stable hands were mucking out while others took horses for turnout.

"This is the main stable," Suzy gestured with her hand, "we have barn help for mucking out and maintenance, but in a pinch, you'll be required to help out in that department too. You okay with that?"

"Sure. I take care of that at home, so once I understand your system it won't be a problem. We use shavings at home for the most part," she added.

Suzy nodded. "Straw's a bit different, but you shouldn't have an issue with it." She moved on. "This is the tack room. Each horse has their own tack." She pointed to the neat rows of saddles and bridles, stack of clean numnahs and saddle pads on a long counter down the middle of the room. Four-pronged hooks hung from the ceiling over the counter. "Tack gets cleaned after each use. Rags, sponges, leather oil, saddle soap, anything you'll need is in the drawers under the counter. Washer and dryer are next to the washrooms which are in the corner there."

"It looks pretty efficient." Laurel scanned the room, noting the rolls of leg wraps and cottons neatly stored on shelves at the end wall.

"Do you have any experience with calks? If not, I'll get Miriam to show you." Suzy turned to face Laurel.

"I know you use different corks for changing conditions. I don't have any on my own horse, but I've groomed for my coach a few times and managed to change the grass corks for the mud ones. I'm not quick at it yet," she admitted.

"Good to know. I appreciate you being honest. We'll get you up to speed and Miriam or I will quiz you on what ones to use in what conditions. At a competition I need to be able to count on you to know and anticipate the needs of both horse and rider."

"I'll do my very best for you." Laurel swallowed the dread in her throat. *What if I screw up? Shit, what if I'm not good enough?*

Suzy laughed and cuffed her gently on the shoulder. "Don't look so scared. You'll be fine. I've had a few talks with your coach and she's confident you'll fit right in. It takes time to learn new skills and routines and we'll give you that time. Within reason," she added.

"Thanks, that helps." Laurel smiled.

"Okay, onward." Suzy led the way past the tack room and out the end door of the stable. "The turnouts are over there. Behind them are the pastures where some of the ponies and school horses live outside all year round." She pointed to a large sand ring where both stadium jumps and dressage markers were stored under a long open but covered area adjacent to the boards. "This is the outdoor ring. We use it most of the time unless it's tipping down. If you use any of the equipment it has to be stored again once you're done, unless you are specifically asked to leave it where it is."

"Okay." Laurel nodded, storing the information, and hoping she wouldn't forget something important. *I should have brought a notebook. Damn it.*

"Don't worry too much about remembering everything, you'll shadow Miriam for the first few days until you get used to the routine," Suzy said, as if reading her thoughts.

"Thanks."

"The indoor is on the other side of the stables, there is actually a covered walkway halfway down that side of the stables that goes directly to the arena." Suzy checked the time on her phone. "That's the basic layout. Any questions so far?"

"I don't think so...well I guess...what time do you want me to start in the mornings? Do I have any days off?" Laurel was hesitant to ask too many questions and make a poor impression.

"Good questions." Suzy nodded. "Let's go back to the office and get those few papers signed. I need to take a copy of your work visa for the records, get you to sign some forms so I can pay you. We'll do over your schedule while we're taking care of that."

On the way back through the stables they stopped for Suzy to introduce Laurel to the stable hands, Celia, Rory, Carlo, and Sandy. Laurel hoped she had the names attached to the right faces. It took only a few minutes to get the paperwork out of the way once they reached the office.

Suzy leaned back in her chair, sunlight gleaming on the trophies in the glass case behind her. "Want some tea? A fizzy drink?" She got up and poured tea from a carafe sitting on a small fridge beside the desk.

"No, I'm good," Laurel said.

Suzy sank back into her chair. "So then. Your work hours are eight to four most days. When there's a competition those times may become significantly longer. You'll be required to help with schooling the horses, at first that may just be hacking out with the ones on a day off, braiding for shows, loading the horse van, making sure everything is in its place. There's nothing more maddening then getting somewhere and finding that what is needed got left at home. You'll have help with that of course, but still part of your responsibilities. You'll ride every day, in all kinds of conditions. If I think you're up for it, you'll take on some of the beginner pupils. Your coach assured me you had experience with the Pony Club in Canada, teaching the E's and D's."

"I really like working with the kids. They're so eager to learn. Although it can be challenging sometimes because of the difference in their horses."

Suzy steepled her fingers and regarded Laurel. "How so?"

"Some of the kids have pretty nice horses, but some of them are on older animals or cranky ponies. Because we don't have large numbers in our club, you end up with widely different calibres of mounts in each class, so I have to create lesson plans that cater to each rider's strengths and weaknesses. It's not so hard with the E's, but the D's are a much wider age and experience differential."

Suzy nodded and seemed pleased with her answer, so Laurel breathed a mental sigh of relief. Suzy got to her feet, gathering the papers, and sticking them in a file folder that went into her desk drawer. She checked the time again.

"I have a lesson in twenty minutes. Go get your boots and I'll have Miriam assign you a mount. We'll see how you fare."

Laurel got to her feet. "I get to ride today?"

"What I just said. I'll text Miriam to meet you at the tack room. Go."

A wide grin split Laurel's face, fueled by the excitement churning in her chest. *I'm in Cornwall and I'm going to get to ride an English horse. Oh my God."*

"Thanks, Suzy. I'll get my boots and meet Miriam." She all but danced out of the office. Retrieving her boots she hurried down the wide aisle to the tack room. Miriam wasn't there yet, but three girls were there gathering up tack. Laurel gauged their ages to be between fifteen and her own age.

"Hi, I'm Laurel. I'm new, but I think I'm going to be in your lesson."

"Hey Laurel, I'm Janet," one of the girls said. "Where are you from? Your accent is weird."

"Canada," Laurel replied.

"Oh good, not the US. I'm Vicki." The dark-haired girl shifted the saddle onto her hip and slipped a bridle over her shoulder.

"What kind of lesson is this one?" Laurel asked. "Flat or over fences?"

"Flat work today, worse luck. I'm Fiona." The red-haired girl grimaced. "I hate flat lessons. Suzy is a devil for correct form, works our arses off."

"Ah, there you are." Miriam breezed into the room. "You three have your assignments, off with you. Laurel, you'll be on Karma. Her tack is here, plain snaffle bridle. Have you ridden in a double bridle at all?"

"No, I've seen them, but I've never ridden a horse that used one," she admitted. "I've used a pelham with double reins but not a real double bridle with the two bits."

"Suzy'll remedy that soon enough, I think. Now, you'd best get a move on. Trust me, you don't want to be late for a lesson. Karma is the chestnut, third stall on the right when you go out the door. Name plate on the door, beside the feeding schedule. Always check the board," she indicated a black board by the door, "that will tell you if your horse needs anything special like bell boots or a girth cover. Karma's good to go, but don't forget to check each time because things change all the time."

Laurel gathered up the equipment, choosing a nice thick lambs' wool numnah to go under the all purpose saddle, and a fitted leather girth. Hurrying her steps she left to find her horse. She only had fifteen minutes left to groom Karma and get tacked up. Pulling up the saddle rack on the front of the stall, she slid the saddle onto it, pad on top and hung the bridle on the hook beside it. A box attached to the open door held brushes and hoof pick. It didn't take more than few minutes work to brush the stable dust off the chestnut mare and pick out her hooves. Being careful not to break hairs, she ran a soft brush down the tail and finger picked any tangles. Glancing out the door, she saw the other girls were tacked up and the red-haired girl—what was her name again—Fiona, was headed out the door. The mare stood quiet while Laurel saddled and bridled her. She slipped out to kick off her Ariats and pull on her beautiful boots that she'd retrieved from the office on her way to the tack room . Thank God for the zipper up the back, her old boots didn't have that luxury and she'd had to use boot pulls to get the darn things on. One last check over the tack, tucking in the loose ends of the bridle into the keepers and checking the length of the throatlatch and noseband, she led the horse out of the stall. She followed Vicki with Janet falling in behind.

Suzy arrived just as the four horses entered the outdoor ring. Miriam already stood in the centre. Laurel took Karma to the middle of the area, checked her girth, ran down her stirrups and double checked everything with the bridle was as it should be. She waited beside Karma's shoulder, copying what the other three were doing. Suzy went to each pair and did a cursory check of the tack and the riders' turnout. When she came to Laurel, she spent more time going over everything. Nodding, she turned and joined Miriam. Laurel swung up into the saddle and gathered her reins, glad she'd remembered to tuck her gloves into her boot bag last night. At Suzy's command, Laurel put Karma on the rail behind the other three.

They worked the horses on a long rein at a free trot, allowing them to move freely and stretch the muscles in their back. After moving in both directions of the ring, they gathered their reins and brought the horses to working trot. Karma had a longer stride than Laurel was used to and was more forward in her movement. Laurel made slight adjustments with her seat and reins to keep the mare from falling onto the forehand. She followed across the diagonal as they changed the rein. On cue, all four horses picked up a canter. After a few circuits of the ring with Suzy making adjustments to their pace and the riders' position, they changed the rein again across the diagonal with a simple change of lead in the centre.

Laurel settled into Karma's gaits and allowed herself a tiny smile. So far so good. They brought the horses back to a walk and gave them a loose rein to allow them to rest while Suzy explained what she wanted next. Keeping the reins in one hand, Laurel slid her feet out of the stirrups and crossed them over the horse's withers in front of the saddle bow. She made sure to cross the left stirrup over last, something her coach had instilled in her. If she needed to get off with the use of a stirrup or get back on, then the left one should be on top. Back out on the rail they went. First at a walk, while Suzy corrected their positions, encouraging them to be sure their horses were tracking up, placing the rear hoof either in front of where the front hoof had landed or beyond it. She explained to Laurel this was to ensure the horse's hind end was engaged and they were allowing their back muscles to swing. She nodded in acknowledgement, her coach at home had already schooled her in that exercise.

They moved up to trot, Laurel sat easily to Karma's trot which was thankfully smooth and rhythmic. Suzy moved her attention from one pupil to the next, asking them to call out which pair of the horse's legs were moving forward. Then it was Laurel's turn.

"Do you know the sequence of legs at the trot?" Suzy tapped out a rhythm on her boot with her crop.

"Outside hind, inside fore together, inside hind, outside fore together," Laurel replied.

"Call your horse for me," Suzy commanded.

Laurel checked to be sure waiting for the pull in her outside hip and the dip in her inside seat bone to tell her which pair of legs was moving forward. "Do you want me to call the front or the hind?" she asked.

"Hind."

"Left, right, left, right," she chanted.

"Now call the forelegs," Suzy challenged her.

Again Laurel chanted the rhythm.

"Well done, now all walk on." Suzy moved back to stand with Miriam.

"Oh God," Fiona moaned as she moved her mount up beside Laurel as the horses took a breather. "Now we're in for it."

"What do you mean?" Laurel kept an eye on the instructor.

"She's in one of her technical moods. You wait, it's gonna be rising trot without stirrups next."

"I've only done that a couple of times at home. I hope I can manage it."

"You better, because she'll keep us at it until we all get it."

"Prepare to trot on." Suzy moved back toward the rail, the better to watch her pupils come toward her, gauging their balance and position in relation to the horse's centre of gravity.

Laurel nudged Karma into a trot, letting her hips swing with the motion. She ran a hand up and down the mare's neck. *What a nice horse.* "Good girl," she whispered.

"Prepare to trot rising and go," Suzy's voice carried over the beat of hooves on the packed track on the rail.

Ahead of her, Janet struggled to keep in sync with her gelding's movement. Fiona looked flawless on the big dark bay, while Vicki missed a couple of beats and got herself onto the wrong diagonal. Laurel tensed her core and rose to Karma's even pace. Thank God she didn't have the kind of gait that lacked cadence and rhythm. They circled the ring twice and Laurel's thighs were starting to burn. Suzy hadn't singled her out for anything but tiny corrections so far, so she was either doing okay or Suzy thought she was hopeless. Poor Janet and Vicki got the bulk of the attention. Fiona shot Laurel a grin across the ring as they passed and gave her a tiny thumbs up. Laurel grinned back and then forced herself to keep moving with Karma. Her calves were complaining now, along with her thighs and the small of her back. She grit her teeth and kept going, being careful not to land on Karma's back with any force but to keep rising in time with her horse.

When she was sure she couldn't keep up a second longer, sweat running down her back and from under her helmet, Suzy called them back to walk. Laurel half-halted Karma to signal a change and then sat and closed her seat to bring her smoothly from trot to walk. It was all she could do not to lean forward and rest on the horse's neck. Instead she adjusted her seat slightly, lengthening her leg and pushing her heels further down. Damn that tendency to pinch with her knees when she got tired.

Suzy checked her watch and consulted with Miriam about something. Laurel didn't much care what at this point. *God, I'm going to be sore when this is over.* Karma blew through her nose but stayed light on the bit in Laurel's hand. A bit of sweat foamed on her neck where the rein rubbed. Suzy let them take back their stirrups and after a bit of canter and some work on flying changes, she concluded the lesson.

"Laurel, come and see me in the office once you've taken care of your horse," Suzy said as she left the ring with Miriam.

"Yes, I'll be there as soon as I can." Laurel swallowed a lump in her throat as she slid off her horse and ran up her stirrups before loosening the girth a couple of notches. Taking the reins over Karma's head, she undid the flash noseband and tucked the long loose ends under the cavesson noseband. "Do you think I'm in trouble?" she asked Fiona who came up beside her as they walked toward the stables.

"I don't think so, Suzy probably just wants to go over a few things. You rode really well. Karma doesn't like people who don't ride well, she can be a right bitch if you get on her wrong side."

Laurel ran a hand down the mare's neck as she walked placidly beside her. "Really? She was awesome, I swear she knew what I was going to ask her before I did it."

Fiona grinned. "Like I said, you did well for your first ride on a strange horse."

* * *

"Suzy?" Laurel tapped on the office door.

"Come in, find a chair." Suzy waved at a couple of chairs that had various pieces of equipment hanging off them.

Laurel perched on the edge of one and taking in the awards and certificates framed on the walls. "You wanted to see me?"

"Just a sec." Suzy looked at a text message that just binged. Smiling, she looked up. "I think you'll do just fine, Laurel Rowan. Miriam confirmed what I expected, that you looked after your horse first, cleaned your tack and put it where it belongs and then double checked on your horse before coming to see me. You did well on Karma, she doesn't suffer fools gladly. If you or your coach had misrepresented your skill, Karma would have betrayed you within the first half-hour of the lesson. I'll see you bright and early tomorrow morning."

"Thanks. See you tomorrow." Laurel recognized the dismissal and got to her feet, aware of the ache in her thighs and groin, not to mention her lower back. She left the inner office and picked up her boots where she left them when she came in from the stables. Pulling a cloth out of the bag she wiped the boots down before tucking them into the bag. *I'll clean them tonight after dinner.* Stepping out into the sunlight, she leaned on the wall, soaking in the warmth and called Sairie. In no time at all, the blue Volkswagen tore up the lane and halted in front of the office. Laurel put her boot bag in the back and collapsed into the front seat.

"How was your unofficial first day?" Sairie asked, putting the car in gear, turning, and heading toward the tarmac road.

"Good." Laurel rested her head on the back of the seat. "I got to ride today, and it was great. A really nice horse. Suzy seemed pleased, so that's a good thing." She tilted her head to smile at Sairie.

"Ready for supper? I've got the makings for fried fish and chips waiting at home."

"That sounds amazing, I'm starving." She pulled her phone out of her pocket as it vibrated. "Coll," she said in response to Sairie's raised eyebrow.

"Should I make enough for three for supper?"

"He wants to come by after he gets off work, but he says he's working until seven-thirty, so I think it's just us for supper. I need to clean up. Every muscle in my body is aching, Suzy made us do rising trot without stirrups for what seemed like forever." She groaned and closed her eyes. "I haven't worked that hard in ages."

"But you managed, and your boss was pleased you said." Sairie turned up the lane to her cottage.

"True." Laurel dragged herself out of the car and snagged her boots out of the back. "It could have been worse. I could have got dumped in the middle of the ring. As it is, I just hurt like hell."

Sairie laughed. "You'll feel better with a full stomach. And you can have a nice visit with Coll after."

Chapter Seven

Laurel put the last plate in the cupboard and hung the dish rag on the rack to dry. She glanced out the window at the crunch of tires outside. Coll got out and turned toward the house, sunlight gleaming off his blond hair.

"Coll's here," Laurel called over her shoulder to Sairie who was shoving laundry into the small machine in the mud room.

"Have fun, you. But remember, morning comes early." The older woman stuck her head into the kitchen, mischief dancing in her blue eyes. "I can well remember what it was like to be young. Times runs differently when you're still just tasting life, but it runs all the same mind you when the cock crows in the morning. Go on, with you." Sairie waved a small towel at Laurel. "I've just got a few more things to fold and then I'm planning on getting started on that new book I got in Penzance at that place on Chapel Street."

"Thanks, Sairie." Laurel gave her a quick hug in passing before opening the door for Coll. "Hey." She stepped outside, pulling the door shut behind her. "What do you want to do?"

"This." Coll pulled her into his chest and settled his lips on hers.

Laurel leaned into him, but when he deepened the kiss, she took a step back. "Besides, that." She smiled to take the sting out of her actions.

Coll lifted a shoulder in a half-hearted shrug, keeping her hand in his. "Want to go get a coffee at the Copper Spoon or Chapel Rock? Or ice cream, maybe?"

"Sure, that sounds nice. I love looking over at St. Michael's Mount. Let's go to the one nearest the beach. That's Chapel Rock, right? Will the tide be out?"

"Not sure about the tide, I haven't checked the charts today. Why?"

"I know it's too late to go out to the island, but if the tide is out, I'd like to just walk along the cobbles of the causeway for a bit." Laurel slid into the car, remembering almost too late to get in the left side rather than the right.

"If that's what you want." Coll joined her, sending a sidelong glance of puzzlement at her. "You really want to go walk on those slippery stones when the light is fading?" He put the car in gear and managed a tight turn to avoid reversing down the narrow lane.

"I do." Laurel bounced sideways in her seat as far as the seat belt would allow. "It's one of my favourite memories. Going out there, all four of us, and then getting to meet Corm." She settled back into her seat, thoughts turned inward for a moment. "Have you ever seen him since?"

Coll shook his head. "No, I never see anything weird unless I'm with you or Aisling. I don't envy Gort marrying her. That little annoying piskie just pops up unexpectedly all the time."

"Gwin Scawen! Oh, I hope I get to see him again." She frowned at Coll. "Why do you think he's annoying? I just think he's cute and funny." Laurel giggled. "I mean, remember how he and his buddies chased Gort's uncle down the street when he was out there raving?"

"I remember." Coll snorted. "But I just don't trust the *pobel vean*. They can turn on you as quick as they can be helpful. I've seen how things can go wrong if they take a dislike to ya. I mean, I live with Gramma, remember? People come to her for help when things go wrong."

60

"What did you call them? I don't think I've heard that term before." Laurel swung her hair behind her ear.

"*Pobel vean*, it means 'little people' in the old tongue. Gramma and Sairie call them that."

"Why?" She frowned as they drove down into Marazion heading for Kings Road. The setting sun sent slanting rays from the west across the waters of Mounts Bay. Laurel's eye drawn to the imposing sight of the castle perched on the top of St. Michael's Mount.

"Sairie and Gramma both say it's best not to call them, as a whole, by a proper name, you don't want to bring unwanted attention to you, now do you?" Coll shook his head. "It never ends well. I'll tell you that."

"You mean I shouldn't call Gwin Scawen by name? But he's my friend," Laurel protested.

Coll sighed and parked in front of the Chapel Rock Café. "I don't know for sure. You know I don't like to meddle in those affairs. That's for Ash, and Gramma and Sairie..." he paused and glanced at her, "...and you I guess. What with your grandfather bein' a selkie and all, and your Gramma Bella living in the other worlds with him most of the time." He suppressed the shiver that crawled across his skin.

"Hmmm, maybe. I guess." Laurel swung her legs out of the car, conscious of the pull of sore muscles. She looked across the sand toward the castle. "Do the St. Aubyn's still live there?"

"They do," Coll replied, taking her hand and drawing her toward the café.

"I can't imagine living someplace like that." She stopped to watch as lights bloomed in the gathering dusk in the windows of the castle, gleaming through and above the trees.

"Not somethin' I've ever thought about." Coll towed her toward the entry to the shop. "Let's get our drinks and then we can do whatever you want."

"Coll, hallo!" The young woman behind the counter greeted him with a brilliant smile which dimmed a bit when she noticed Laurel.

"Hallo, Lily. How'ev ye been." He turned toward Laurel. "You remember Laurel, right? She stayed with Sairie when her mom was sick, went to school with us for a bit."

"Yeah, sure. I remember. Hi Laurel, you visiting for a week or two?" She wiped the counter with a clean cloth, eyes skipping from Coll to Laurel.

"Actually, no. I'm here for a bit longer. I've got a position with Suzie Wish at Longrock Equestrian as a working student." Laurel glanced up at the menu board, puzzled by the undercurrent evident in the woman's voice.

"Oh, well then." Lily set the cloth down with a bit more force than seemed necessary. "What can I get for you two, then?"

Armed with a mocha latté, Laurel turned toward the door. Coll waited at the counter for the biscuits he'd ordered.

"I'll wait for you outside." Laurel pushed the door open with her free hand and moved to watch the tide encroach on the cobbled walkway leading out to the tidal island.

"Right, I won't be long." Coll leaned a hip on the counter.

After a while, Laurel realized the tide covered most of the walkway now. She glanced toward the café. *I wonder what's keeping him.* Moving to put her empty cup in the bin, she glanced through the shop window and stopped in her tracks. Coll was leaning across the narrow counter inside holding both of Lily's hands. To Laurel's surprise, he released one of her hands to wipe something off her cheek. *What the hell is that about?* Her stomach clenched as suspicion reared its head. Was something going on between Coll and Lily? If he had something going with her, why was he pushing Laurel so hard to make some kind of commitment she

62

wasn't ready for? Laurel crushed the cardboard cup and threw it into the bin before shoving the shop door open and sticking her head in.

"Are you coming? I've finished my latté and I really need to get back. I've got an early morning."

Coll spun around; his face flushed. Lily busied herself wiping down the already clean counter, avoiding looking at either of them.

"Oh, sorry. I was waiting for the biscuits." He picked up the bag from the counter.

Laurel raised an eyebrow at him. "Well, looks like you've got them now. I'll be at the car. If you're not there in five, I'm calling Sairie to come get me." Laurel shut the door and went to lean on the fender of Coll's car. She pulled out her phone and brought up Sairie's contact. Four minutes passed, her finger hovered over the call icon, the muscles in her jaw taut with annoyance.

"Sorry, sorry." Coll rushed up out of breath, the paper bag clutched in his hand. "Want one?" He held the biscuits toward her.

"Half an hour ago." Laurel kept a tight rein on her rising anger.

"Yeah, sorry." He unlocked the car doors and got in, setting the biscuit bag on the tiny console between the seats.

Laurel joined him, being careful not to look at him. From the corner of her eye she caught Coll looking toward her and opening his mouth, then closing it. He hit the ignition and backed the car out onto the roadway. The short drive to Sairie's cottage was made in strained silence. Coll pulled up by the mudroom door and turned the car off. He made to open his door to get out.

"Don't bother coming in, I've got stuff I need to do and then I really need to get some sleep." Laurel got out and closed the door with more force than was necessary, muffling whatever it was Coll was saying. Without a backward glance, she walked the short distance to the door and slipped inside, closing the door firmly behind her.

"What the hell," she muttered. "What has he been up to that nobody's told me about?" Shaking her head, she pushed through the door into the kitchen.

"I just wet the tea when I saw lights coming up the lane." Sairie set the old blue pottery tea pot on the table along with three mugs.

Laurel threw herself into the nearest chair, resting her elbows on the table. "Coll's not coming in." Restless, she got up and took the extra mug back to the cupboard.

"Something amiss?" Sairie narrowed her eyes at the younger woman.

"Something or someone?" Laurel clenched her jaw and sat back at the table.

"Whatever does that mean? Something you want to talk about or are you just planning on staring holes in my teapot?"

"Coll, what's Coll been up to around here? I thought we were good, I mean I know this long-distance thing isn't great, but I thought it was working." The words burst out of Laurel. She moved her gaze from the teapot to Sairie's face. "Do you know who he's been hanging around with?"

"Well now," Sairie chose her words carefully, "of course, Gort and Aisling just like always. Stuart's been around a fair bit according to Emily, and sometimes that cousin of his, Lily, comes along with him. Why do you ask, my love? You're teasy as an adder tonight."

Laurel snorted through her nose. "I'm pissed because Coll took me out for coffee and then spent the whole time leaning on the counter in the shop talking to Lily...and holding her hands. Like she was upset about something. When she saw me walk in, it was like something horrible just happened. Her face went white, and she wouldn't even look at me." She reached across and gripped Sairie's hand. "Is there something going on between Coll and her? Have I been an idiot back home thinking we were in a relationship?"

"I don't see your bunch as much as I used to when you were living here so I'm not really in a position to know what Coll, or Lily for that matter, are up to in the village, or in Penzance. I can ask Emily what she thinks, if you like."

Laurel flung herself back in her chair. "I don't know. I just don't know. It sure seemed like there was more than casual friendship between them. What if Emily tells Coll you were asking and ...oh.. I don't know..."

"Maybe the best thing would be to talk to Coll about it. See what he has to say and that might put your mind at rest. At the very least you should have a better idea of the lay of the land." Sairie poured milk into one of the cups and then added the hot tea. "Drink your tea. Everything looks better after a good cuppa." She pushed the full mug toward Laurel and made one for herself.

The two women sat in the pool of light, each lost in their own thoughts while the night pushed against the window. After a long silence, Laurel rose and took her mug to the sink where she rinsed it and set it on the sideboard. She turned and hugged Sairie over the back of her chair.

"Thanks, Sairie. Maybe things will look better in the morning. I'm headed for bed."

"Be sure you have that talk with Coll." Sairie squeezed her hand.

"I will." Laurel left the kitchen and felt her way up the narrow dark staircase to her bedroom door off the tiny landing. She cleaned and polished her riding boots before changing for bed. Dim starlight fell across the bed when she crawled into it. After tossing and turning for ten minutes that seemed like hours, she drew her knees up and leaned against the headboard. Without thinking too much about it, she picked up her phone and texted Aisling.

:Hey what's the deal with Coll and Lily?:

:?:

Laurel held her breath for a second before replying. Not at all sure she really wanted to know the answer.
:Do they hang out a lot together?:

:Sure, some.:

Aisling was dancing around answering the question. Frustrated, Laurel hit the call icon. It was easier to find out what she wanted actually talking to Ash.

"Hey, Laurel. It's late, is something wrong?"

"You tell me, Ash. Quit avoiding my question. Is there something going on between Coll and Lily? For God's sake tell me if there is."

There was a long silence before Aisling spoke. " Lily's been coming around with Stuart the last six months or so. She's close with Stuart and I guess that's how it started. Lately, she's been showing up on her own ... I don't think Coll's telling her where we'll be, but I don't know ...I'm sorry, Laurel. I didn't think it was anything serious or I would have told you. You really think there might be something between them?"

"Based on what I saw tonight, I think there might be. I don't want to think it, Ash! I've always trusted Coll."

"Long distance is hard, Laurel. There's concerts and all kinds of stuff where it's nice to have someone to go with. And especially with me and Gort being a couple, Coll must feel left out sometimes."

"I know, it's the same for me. Carly and Joey are always together, and sometimes it's just so tempting to let Chance come along and make it a foursome. But I don't encourage him, that's for sure." Laurel clenched her jaw. "It sure as hell looked like there was more than casual friendship between Coll and Lily."

66

"Laurel Rowan, you're jealous." There was laughter in Aisling's voice.

"Of course, I'm jealous! I thought Coll and I had an understanding, maybe I was wrong." Laurel gripped the phone harder.

"Do you want me to talk to Gort about it? See if Coll's confided in him or said anything about Lily?"

"I don't know, Ash. That seems kinda sneaky. Maybe I should just take the bull by the horns and ask him straight out. Damn it! I hate not knowing what to do."

"Let me know if want me to ask G." Aisling yawned. "I've got the early shift at the shop tomorrow, it's time I went to bed."

"Yeah, sorry. I didn't realize how late it was. I have to be up before the sun too. When are we getting together to start planning the wedding? Do they throw bridal showers over here or is that a North American thing? Do I need to organize that and surprise you? Oh, Lord, let's talk about this when we're not both half asleep."

"Let me know what day you have off soon and I'll make sure I have it off too. We can get together with Sairie and Emily and get things moving." Aisling smothered another yawn.

"What about your mom? Doesn't she want to be part of it?"

"Mum wants nothing to do with me marrying Gort. Bad blood she says. Nothing good can come of it. Utter nonsense, but there you go," Aisling sounded resigned.

"God, I'm sorry Ash. I can't imagine planning my wedding without my mom."

"At least Dad's agreed to help us pay for the food. Emily's making over a wedding dress that was her mother's for me. So that's something."

"Do you like the dress? I mean we could go shopping for a new one if you wanted, my treat," Laurel offered, figuring she could dip into the money Gramma Bella left her.

"That's so sweet, but honestly, I love the dress. And Emily is so happy that it will get some use as she wore it on her wedding day. I'm so lucky that Emily and Coll let us move in here when Mum laid down the law. Either I dump Gort, or I move out."

"That's pretty harsh. I'm sorry, Ash."

"I've learned to live with it. It's not like Mum and me were ever really close like you and your mum. She's always been wary of me since she figured out my imaginary friends weren't so imaginary. She caught me talking to Gwin Scawen when I was about ten. When she couldn't smack the demons, as she called them, out of me it's been awkward between us ever since." Aisling snorted. "She even asked the priest to do an exorcism, if you can believe it."

"She didn't! Did the priest go through with it?" Laurel was appalled.

"Thankfully, no. But it was bloody close. Dad put his foot down and forbid it."

"When did she try that? Like when you were ten?"

"Oh, no. After the first few incidents I learned to hide my dealings with the Otherworld. No, she decided exorcism was the only way to save me when I told her Gort and I were planning to get married once I turned eighteen. Emily and Sairie were livid, they both went and talked to Dad, who had no idea what Mum was about. That put paid to it, but I decided I needed to get out of the house and Mum solved that for me by kicking me out. Short version of long story."

"I wish I'd been here to help you. Being so far away really sucks." Laurel played with a strand of hair before tucking it behind her ear.

Aisling chuckled. "You could always just marry Coll and come live here for good, That'd solve the problem. And put Lily in her place."

"It's not that simple, Ash."

"I know, lovey. Let's talk about this tomorrow after work. I've got to get some sleep. Night."

"Sounds like a plan. Night, Ash." Laurel ended the call and set the phone on the quilt by her knees. She slid down in the bed, but it was a long time before sleep came.

Chapter Eight

Laurel rolled out of bed, taking a moment to look out across the meadow, the horses dim shapes in the pre-dawn glow. Satisfied all were accounted for, she made short work of her morning wash and pulled on riding clothes. Slinging her boot bag over her shoulder, she padded down the steep stairs and into the kitchen. Setting the boots by the door, Laurel rummaged in the fridge for some butter, snagged two scones from the covered plate, then smeared them with the butter. Cramming them into her mouth, she put the butter dish back in the fridge, grabbed the bagged lunch and pushed open the mud room door. Laurel shoved her feet into her work boots, picked up the boot bag along with a knapsack which she shoved the lunch bag into along with three bottles of water, and slipped out the door.

"Oh!" The figure on the path just outside the door stopped her short.

"Morning, my love." Sairie shifted the basked of eggs to her other hand and gave Laurel a one-armed hug. "Off already, are ye? You know I don't mind giving you a lift, just let me put the eggs inside."

"No, I need to start being more independent. I don't expect you to drive me every day. I've got the bike and I actually enjoy the quiet time. It'll give me a chance to think. Figure things out..." Laurel's voice trailed off and she stepped away from the older woman.

"Things that would include Coll and that tall cowboy back home?" Sairie fixed her with a shrewd gaze.

"Not that so much, it's...well it's more about Coll and Stuart's cousin."

"Lily? You still stewing about that this morning?" Sairie's eyebrows rose in surprise.

Laurel shrugged. "I guess I am, after I talked to Ash about it last night."

"Aye, I know seeing her and Coll so cozy was upsetting last night?" She shifted the basket of eggs to rest on her hip.

"I hate being so suspicious, I'm sure I'm just being silly, but it seemed like there was more than just casual friendship between them. Especially on her end."

"Have you spoken to Coll about this?"

"Not yet, but I will tonight. Right now, I need to get going or I'll be late. See you at supper."

She glanced back toward the cottage when she threw her leg over the bike after tucking the bags into the carrier. Sairie was still standing by the mud room door, the first rays of sunlight throwing a halo around her head. Laurel waved and pushed off down the lane.

Twenty minutes later, she bumped up the lane of the stable yard. Parking the bike, she entered the side door of the stables, bypassing the office. In the tack room, she put her lunch in the small fridge and set her boot bag inside her locker. Checking her appearance in the mirror over the sink, she smoothed her hair and straightened her shirt. Suzie insisted her staff was neat and presentable at all times and Laurel made sure she followed the rules. It was still early days yet. The last thing she needed was to get sent home.

"Mornin'," she called stepping into the barn proper, a pitchfork fork in her hand.

"Morning, Laurel," Fiona replied. She dipped the scoop into the feed cart and decanted the contents into the grain bin of the horse beside her. "I got in early so the feeding is almost done. Vicki and Janet are checking the pasture horses, so if you don't mind can you start turning out the ones who've finished eating?

The list of horses we need left in is on the whiteboard by the tack room." Fiona went back to her duties.

"Of course." Laurel checked the names listed on the board before going to the other end of the long aisle where most of the horses were sticking their heads out over the stall guards.

"Looks like you guys have finished breakfast." She ran a hand down the sleek neck of the horse nearest her. The head collars and leads hung on hooks on the front of each stall, making it quick work to transfer the twelve horses who weren't in use for the morning out to their paddocks. On her way back to the barn after latching the gate of the last paddock she was joined by Janet and Vicki.

"All is as it should be with the pasture horses," Janet said, falling into step with Laurel.

"Ah, that should be the barn crew," Vicki said at the growl of the tractor coming to life. "It's a bonus that Suzy has extra staff to take care of the mucking out. A lot of places get the most they can out of the working students and work them like dogs. Mucking out, repairs. The last place I was at was murder, plain and simple. I'm so grateful Suzy offered me a spot with her."

Laurel smiled. "It is nice not to have to muck out every day, but honestly, at home I kinda like mucking out. But from what I've seen of the schedule here, we're gonna be running our butts off once the shows start."

"Next week." Janet grinned. "I can't wait. It'll just be grooming for the first while, but Suzy promised we'd get to participate too. I so want to take on the course at Badminton."

"As if." Vicki smacked her lightly on the shoulder. "Badminton is the big time. I'm just excited to get to be part of it. Behind the scenes and away from the crowd. We'll get to walk the cross-country course with Suzy and the others."

"It's only a couple of weeks away, I'm so glad I got here before." Laurel followed the other girls into the stable.

"Let's see what Suzy has planned for us today." Fiona gestured at the whiteboard by the tack room. The others gathered around her to get their assignments for the day.

"Oh, look, look! I can't believe it," Janet squealed. She turned and flung her arms around Vicki, dancing in place.

"What is it?" Laurel craned her neck trying to see what set the girl off into such raptures.

"It's the best assignment ever. We're taking the horses down to the beach at Long Rock to give them a swim in the bay," Fiona informed her. "The tide will be in by the time we ride down there, so let's get a move on."

The four girls gathered up bridles and hurried to their assigned mounts. Laurel was pleased to see she had Karma again. The chestnut mare stood quietly while she brushed her down. By the time Laurel set the last hoof down and replaced the hoof pick in the brush box by the stall door, the others were in the process of bridling their horses. Without wasting any time, Laurel slid the bridle on the chestnut and followed the others out to the mounting block. Within seconds all four girls were astride, just as they turned toward the gate Miriam trotted up on a tall bay stallion. He arched his neck and snorted when she reined him in.

"Ready for a swim?" Miriam sat easily on the muscular Thoroughbred.

"You're coming with us?" Janet asked.

Miriam nodded. "Suzy wants this lad to get more comfortable around other horses and a splash in the bay should take some of the ginger out of him." She grinned and slid a hand up and down the shiny curved neck.

"What fun." Fiona laughed. "He's gorgeous. I haven't had much of a chance to get to know him since Suzy brought him home last week."

"He's settling in as well as can be expected. Let's set out before he decides to do some mischief." Miriam led the way toward the bridle path, the big bay tossed his head and danced a little as they set off single file.

Laurel let Karma pick her place in line which was just behind Fiona and Miriam. The late April sun filtered through the leaves overhead throwing dappled shadows and glinting patches of light on the sandy footing. A light breeze lifted Karma's mane and brushed Laurel's cheeks as she settled into the mare's long stride. With one eye on keeping a safe distance from Fiona's gelding in front of her, Laurel let her thoughts wander. Mom would love this trail, overhung with arched branches of trees and the sweet scent of wild flowers perfuming the air. She smiled and pushed back the tiny spurt of homesickness. So far everything was living up to her expectations when she decided to come to Cornwall. Well, except maybe for the situation with Coll. On one hand he pushed for some kind of commitment from her she wasn't ready to give and on the other it looked like there was something more than friendship between him and Lily. Laurel shook her head and dismissed the annoying thoughts. Questions without answers didn't have any place in this beautiful morning.

In less time than Laurel expected they reached the long beach that ran from Marazion to Penzance. The waters of Mounts Bay glittered in the early morning sun, a faint mist shimmering over the waves. The sand glowed in the slanted rays, and best of all, most of the sandy beach at the edge of the water was empty. Karma shifted under her, muscles gathering. The mare was familiar with the location and clearly anticipating either a good gallop or a swim. Miriam took the lead and rode into the shallow water. Laurel let Karma pick her own pace, and the mare stepped into the sea undeterred by the waves splashing up her legs. The mare snorted and pawed the water sending huge sprays of water everywhere. With little urging from her rider, the chestnut plunged into the deeper water, wetting Laurel to her thighs. She licked the salt from her lips and let the chose their way through the waves. The other horses spread out around her, Fiona and Miriam in the deeper water where their horses swam with their heads parallel to the water, lips drawn back.

"C'mon, Laurel." Fiona waved a hand in her direction. "Karma loves to swim, don't worry."

"Okay, girl. Let's go for it." Laurel leaned forward and took a handful of mane, letting her legs drift out behind her as the mare surged forward. It was so different from swimming the horses in the river at home. The salt water had considerably more buoyancy than the Old Man River and less current. Although the tide tugged at her legs and the water was chilly, it was wonderful. A laugh of pure joy burst from her throat. Karma shook her head and turned toward the south, bringing the impressive view of Saint Michael's Mount with the castle perched on its apex into Laurel's line of sight. Miriam and Fiona were out farther than Laurel. She set aside her caution of venturing out too far to drink in the beauty of the vista in front of her. *Just wait until I tell Carly about this!* Laurel allowed Karma to swim out and join her stablemates.

"Having fun?" Miriam shot her a brilliant smile.

"Yes! This is amazing." Laurel let her excitement show in her face and voice. "What a perfect morning."

"It is, isn't it?" Fiona came up alongside her. "This is my favourite thing in the whole world."

"I think it's mine too." Laurel laughed.

"It's good for the horses too," Miriam came up on her other side. "Lets us exercise them without putting any strain on the legs. And they love it." She ran a hand up and down the big bay's neck. "He's doing very well for his first time in the water that we know of."

Laurel hid her astonishment. She would have taken more care about introducing the horse to the water for the first time. Her thoughts must have shown on her face, however.

"Ah, you're thinking that I should have taken more care with this fellow," Miriam said shrewdly.

"Well, yeah, I guess I'm a bit surprised, but he seems to be handling it well," Laurel admitted.

"That's why all of you four are with me. He reads the other horses' body language, they're not afraid and they're actually excited about going into the water, so he takes his cue from them. Also, I have the four of you to help in case things got hairy. But he's a brave soul, so he is." Miriam slapped the curved neck lightly; the stallion cocked an ear back at her and shook his head.

By unspoken accord the three riders turned their horses toward the other two splashing about in the shallower water. Janet stood on her horse's back in her bare feet and let herself fall backward over his rump while Vicki held her reins. She surfaced, tossing her hair out of her face and laughing. Janet swam back to her mount and slipped onto his slick back, taking the reins back from Vicki.

"Time to head back," Miriam announced. "Still a lot of work to do yet today." Her mount snorted and nodded his head as if he chose to emphasize her words.

The four horses trotted through the shallow water sending rainbow droplets into the air around them. Laurel was enchanted by the effect, her eyes dazzled for a moment when three little undines leaped out of the waves, summersaulting through the rainbow light trailing tendrils of seaweed behind them. Laurel bit her lip to keep from greeting them. No telling how the other girls would react and the last thing she needed was to set herself apart from them in any way. Not when she was just getting to know them.

The ride home seemed shorter than the ride out, but it was plenty of time for the salt to dry on Laurel's skin and begin to itch. They clattered into the stable yard and slid down from their horses.

"Make sure you wash your horse down well, get the salt out of their coats. Janet and Vicki, use the wash rack in this stable, Fee and Laurel come with me, we'll use the racks over in the stallion yard. We'll meet you back here when we're done." Miriam led the way toward the big row of stalls Laurel hadn't been near yet. "Don't forget to clean those bridles either, ladies," the head girl called over her shoulder.

"We won't," Janet and Vicki chorused together.

Laurel took advantage of the hose pipe to wash herself down as well as Karma. Once Fee and Laurel were done, they took their horses back to the other stable yard. Miriam stayed behind to settle the big horse in his stall before following them.

"That was great fun," Vicki remarked when Laurel and Fee entered the tack room, bridles in hand.

"It was so different than swimming in the river back home, I've never swam a horse in the sea before." Laurel hung her bridle on one of the four-pronged hooks dangling from the ceiling over the counter in the centre of the room. Set about stripping the bridle down to its separate parts, dumping the bit into the pail of warm water in the sink.

"It's always a treat when we get to take the horses for a splash," Fiona applied saddle soap to her reins. "I bet we take the event horses for a long hack this afternoon, some hills to increase their stamina and some controlled gallops."

"Did you check the board when we got back? I didn't think to." Janet fished her bit out of the water and dried it to a shine with a soft cloth.

"Some of the old roads and tracks this afternoon, ladies." Miriam breezed into the tack room, riding helmet in her hand. "Your horses are on the board next to your name. Fee, you know the route, so you take the lead."

"Of course. We'll get on it as soon as we get this tack put away," Fee promised.

"Where are we going?" Laurel asked while making quick work of reassembling the bridle and putting it in its place.

"Overland past Penzance and then on to Lands End. It's ten miles from Penzance to Lands End or thereabouts, and we use the distance from here to Penzance to warm up on the way out and cool down on the way home," Fee explained.

"Let's go see who we got to ride. Oh, I hope I get Rocket." Vicki skipped out the door.

Laurel let Janet and Fee go ahead of her. She peered over their shoulders at the white board. Vicki was in raptures as her name was indeed beside Rocket's. Laurel didn't recognize the name of her horse.

"What's Blue like?" She fell into step beside Fee.

"You'll love him, Laurel. He's a real goer. C'mon, he's over in the event yard with the others."

Laurel crossed the cobbled area between the stables. The tack room was much like the one she was used to in the main horse yard. All the tack neatly stowed on racks with the horse's nameplate displayed on the saddle rack, bridle and breastplate hanging below. She collected the tack and a fleece numnah before stepping into the aisle behind the others.

"Blue's stall is the last one on the left." Fiona waved a helpful hand toward the end of the row where a dark head turned in their direction.

"Thanks." Laurel hurried toward Blue, pulling up the rack on the front of the stall to hold the tack. She slid the head collar and lead on before bringing the gelding out of the stall and hooking the crossties on either side. It was only a moment's work to brush the shining hide and pick out his hooves. Blue stood quietly, but his excitement at an outing showed in his eyes and distended nostrils.

"We'll be at it soon, son. Stand up while I get your things on and we'll be off," Laurel assured him, running a hand down the sleek curve of his neck. She was glad of the mounting block she'd seen coming in, Blue was a good 17.2 hands at the wither. It would make things a lot easier to get on if she didn't have to do it from the ground. While she loved her new boots, the length of them made it hard to bend her leg enough to reach the stirrup of the horse that stood higher than her head. Easing the girth up another notch, she undid the crossties and slide the reins over Blue's head. He helpfully dipped his head and took the bit out of her hand, keeping his head lowered while she slipped the crownpiece over his ears and slipped his forelock free of the browband.

"Ready when you are," she called to the other girls.

In moments the five horses moved out of the stable yard. Fee took the lead with the others single file behind her. The track was level for the first bit but soon followed some gently rolling hills. A swell of contentment swept through Laurel. Sunshine, a light breeze off the bay and a great horse under her. What more could a girl ask. Miriam called for them to pick up the pace now the horses were warmed up. Long periods of trotting interspersed with shorter canters soon settled the horses down. Blue snorted and tossed his head, catching at the bit, asking for more rein. Laurel grinned and held him in check. Miriam's instructions were no galloping. The exercise was to promote stamina and endurance.

The horses came to halt at the brow of a tall hill. The horses gathered around Miriam.

"We'll take a bit of break here. There's a nice track along here where we can ride abreast at a walk." She led the way along a wide path winding down toward a shallow valley. "Quiz time," she called.

"Bloody hell," Janet muttered. "I hate this part."

"What kind of quiz?" Laurel leaned toward the girl riding beside her.

79

"Likely something about eventing I'd wager," Fee said.

"You know Suzy insists her working students understand and appreciate all aspects of eventing. That includes knowing something about the history of the sport. So, it's my duty to educate you." Miriam threw a wicked smile over her shoulder. "Anyone know how the sport of eventing started?"

Laurel glanced at the other girls; she had no idea about the history of eventing. Janet shook her head and fiddled with her reins causing her mare to shake her head hard enough to make the fittings jingle.

"Well?" Miriam prompted.

"Some kind of cavalry, military thing? Like polo?" Fee guessed.

"Good guess. Yes, it was the military. It was originally created to ascertain if a horse was suitable to go into battle. The animal needed to fit, obedient, and most of all have the endurance, stamina, and courage to face the chaos of the battlefield. The original three-day event competition was open only to serving officers. Can one of you name the components of the original trial?"

"Dressage, Cross Country and Stadium jumping," Vicki replied.

"Close, but not everything," Miriam said.

"Didn't they used to do something called Roads and Tracks?" Fee chimed in.

"They did." Miriam turned in her saddle and smiled. "Originally there was the dressage test to measure the level of obedience in the horse, then there was the stamina and courage tests. First, they covered a set distance at trot and canter which was termed Roads and Tracks, this was followed by a short rest, then the horse and rider were required to complete a steeplechase course then another round of Roads and Tracks. After that they were evaluated in the hold box and if the horse's heartrate returned to eighty beats per minute within a set time of ten minutes, they were allowed to tackle the cross-country portion of the trial immediately afterward. The obstacles were pretty harsh compared to modern day ones, steep banks that were almost vertical, wide jumps that could be banked onto or just jumped over depending on the courage and scope of the horse. Water obstacles, jumping both into and out of water. Fences with big drops on the far side. Most of today's obstacles are fashioned after the original tests. The stadium jump course was to determine if the horse could continue in service after passing the obedience, stamina, and courage trials."

"Wow, that's crazy. But I guess if you had to count on your horse to obey you and not get both of you killed in battle, you'd want to be pretty sure of how they would react to crazy things," Laurel mused.

"When did they take the Roads and Tracks and the steeplechase out of the competition?" Janet asked, nudging her horse up beside Miriam's.

"Good question. It was in 2004, at the Athens Olympics. The Federation Equestre Internationale decided to removed the roads and tracks and the steeplechase from the trial."

"Was that to make things easier on the horse and rider now that the military aspect wasn't pertinent anymore, or was it to shorten the length of the competition and reduce costs? Vicki wondered.

"That I don't know. But if you're really curious you could ask Suzy, she most likely will have the answer for you." Miriam picked up her reins now the bridle path leveled out. "Enough lally gagging about, time to put some miles on these beasts."

Laurel gathered up the slack in her reins and touched Blue with her heels. He snorted and picked up his long ground covering trot, surging ahead of Fee's horse, and falling into place behind Miriam.

After covering some miles, Laurel realized they were circling back toward the yard from a different direction. Sweat darkened Blue's coat and a line of white lather marked where the reins lay on his neck.

Her own shirt stuck to her back, perspiration trickling down between her breasts. Adjusting her grip on the reins, she was thankful for the textured gloves. Sweat, both hers and the horse's, made the reins slick.

"Follow me," Miriam called. She turned off the track, jumping a low place in the hedge running alongside. Blue turned with no urging from his rider.

Laurel rose into a half-seat, letting Blue stretch into a controlled canter over the grassy turf. Ahead, was a course of low-level obstacles. Anticipation twisted in her gut. She'd never jumped Blue before and some of the fences were bigger than she was used to. The horse's pace was steady beneath her, his ears pricked forward. Laurel grinned and only just stopped herself from squealing with glee as Blue flowed over the barrel jump and headed toward a solid in and out.

She straightened and shifted her weight back a bit to hold Blue to a safe distance behind Miriam. The obstacle had two options, one a foot higher than the other. Laurel aimed Blue for the lower side, but the big horse had ideas of his own and took the higher side, landing lightly and setting himself up nicely to jump out the other side. After that, Laurel let him choose the line, and before she was ready, Miriam was pulling up on the far side of the field. The last jump was a two-foot-high horizontal log with the landing in a pool of water. The big horse took off and Laurel remembered to lean back before they hit the water, only losing her balance slightly and regaining her right stirrup as he jumped out of the water onto the bank. She brought him down to a trot and then a walk as she joined Miriam, turning her horse to watch the other girls finish the course.

Fee sailed over the rail, landing neatly, and joining them with a huge grin. Vicki came next, pecking down on her horse's neck when they hit the water but coming through unscathed. Janet's eyes were huge as she approached the obstacle, she leaned forward over the log and flipped over her horse's shoulder into the water. The horse continued on, splashing out of the pond, and trotting over to join his stable mates. Laurel caught the dangling reins while Miriam went to help Janet out of the water.

"You forgot to lean back before you hit the water." Miriam offered her hand to haul the dripping girl out of the pond.

"I know, I know. God, I hate water jumps." Janet squelched her way over and took the reins from Laurel.

Miriam gave her a leg up before mounting her own horse that Fee was holding for her. Laurel gave Janet a sympathetic smile as they turned toward home, moving at a slower pace now to cool the horses out before arriving back at the yard. Janet kept her head down, refusing to look at the other girls. Laurel glanced at Fee who lifted a shoulder in a silent shrug.

They horses clattered into the yard. Laurel swung off Blue, loosening his girth and running a hand down his neck. "Good boy," she whispered, "thanks for not dumping me in the pond." She stripped his tack off and slid the head collar on. One of the wash bays was open and she led him in. It took no time to wash him off and then cover him with a light stable rug. Making sure his mane and tail were free of tangles and his hooves were clean, she left him to his hay net. Setting the saddle and pad on her hip, she hooked the bridle and breastplate over her shoulder and headed for the tack room. Fee and Vicki were already there taking their bridles apart. Laurel joined them, putting the pad with the others to be washed in the big machine. She laid the saddle on a rack and removed the stirrup leathers, putting them with the girth and other tack on the counter.

"Where's Janet?" she whispered.

Vicki shook her head.

I think she's in the office with Suzy and Miriam," Fee whispered back.

Laurel's heart gave a start of shock. "She's not in shit, is she? For coming off in the pond?" Her stomach rolled. If Janet was in trouble for falling off, what did that mean? Could you get kicked off the team for one fall?

"Everybody comes off at one point or another," Fee assured her. "Miriam wasn't upset about it. I don't know why she's in there and not out here cleaning her tack." She nodded toward the pile of muddy tack piled on a saddle rack. "Vicki took care of her horse as well as her own." Fee frowned.

"She just left her horse?" Laurel raised her eyebrows, all the while her hands busy soaping and oiling the bridle leather.

Vicki nodded. "She untacked, stomped in here, dumped it and went to talk to Miriam. Next thing we knew, her and Miriam were in the office with Suzy."

"Huh." Laurel tried to wrap her head around the girl abandoning the horse to some else's care instead of looking after him herself. It went against everything Laurel believed in.

Once she'd finished with her own tack, she pitched in to help Fee and Vicki with Janet's tack. By the time they had finished, Janet was still in the office with Suzy. Miriam had disappeared over to the far stable yard to give a lesson to three young girls. Laurel stepped into Blue's stall and pulled the stable rug off. His coat was dry and she spent some time brushing him until he shone, finger combing his mane and long thick tail. Satisfied he was as immaculate as she could make him, she put a clean rug on him and took the damp one into the tack room and added it to the pile waiting to be washed once the washer was free.

Fee fell into step with her on the way back to the yard they usually worked out of. "Long day." She grinned.

"It was awesome. I wasn't expecting to get to jump today. That little course was fun and Blue is amazing. I was just along for the ride." Laurel enthused.

"You did great. That's one of Miriam's little tests. See how we handle unexpected challenges."

84

"Have you seen Janet? She's not still in the office, is she?" Laurel glanced toward the office building.

"I don't think so. But I haven't seen her around either."

The two girls entered the stable and headed to the tack room to collect their belongings. Vicki was already there, changing out of her high boots into muckers.

"Quitting time." She sighed. "I haven't seen Janet, before you ask. I think she went off already."

"We didn't run into her either," Fee replied. "I guess we'll see if she shows up in the morning."

"You don't think they let her go, do you?" Laurel looked up from wiping down her riding boots before putting them in their bag.

"I doubt it," Vicki said. "But she might have quit...I'm not sure how happy she is here."

"Really?" Laurel zipped up the boot bag and slid her feet into sneakers. "How can she not be happy? I mean getting to ride all these great horses and I'm learning so much already..."

"Maybe she's just feeling over faced." Fee shrugged. "I don't know. I think maybe her parents want this for her more than she does. Glad it's not me getting pushed into something."

"That would suck," Laurel agreed.

"Plans for the evening?" Vicki put on a sweater. "Need a ride?"

"I've got my bike, but thanks. No big plans, I think Coll is coming over later."

"Ah, Coll Hazel." Vicki grinned. "I wonder how Lily is taking that." She exchanged a glance with Fee.

"What do you mean? What does Lily have to do with Coll coming over tonight? Is there something going on between them that I don't know about?" Laurel looked from one girl to the other.

"Probably not on his part, Laurel. But Lily...well Lily has had her heart set on Coll since they were kids. When you went back to Canada, she was sure Coll would forget about you. She pestered Stuart to let her tag along every time he hung out with Coll and the others. I don't' think you have anything to worry about." Fee patted her shoulder. "Why don't you talk to him about it?"

"For sure, I will." Laurel frowned. "See you in the morning."

She swung up on her bike and pedaled down the lane, her muscles were sore but in a good way. What a great day! Swimming in the sea and then getting to jump Blue over that little course. The horses were what was important, she decided. The situation with Coll would sort itself out.

Maybe Lily was why he was pushing so hard to get a commitment out of Laurel. Or maybe it was knowing that Gort and Aisling were getting married soon. Fee and Sairie were right, she really needed to talk to Coll about all this.

Chapter Nine

Laurel turned into Sairie's laneway, careful to avoid the rut at the end, and breathed a sigh of relief. A shower would be heaven and some clean clothes. But what a day! What a day! She skidded to a halt, dismounted, and unslung the boot bag from her shoulder, before leaning the bike on the side of the shed. Her hand on the latch of the cottage, she swung around at the sound of a car coming up the lane. *Damn it, Coll.* He wasn't supposed to show up for another hour. He must have got off work early. Instead of waiting, Laurel ducked through the door and went through into the kitchen.

"Hello, lovey. Good day, was it?" Sairie looked up from the counter where she was scrubbing vegetables.

"The best. But Sairie, Coll's just coming up the lane and I need a shower. Do you mind occupying him while I scrape some of this dirt off?"

"Of course. I expect he's bringing Emily and Aisling with him." She laughed at the expression on Laurel's face. "You've forgotten that we're getting together tonight to plan the wedding, haven't you?"

"Damn it, yes, I did forget. I need to get Coll alone for a bit at some point tonight. Can you help?"

"Sounds serious. Of course, I'll do what I can. Now off with you and scrape that dirt off." Sairie dried her hands on a dishcloth.

Laurel slipped into the narrow hall, closing the door on the sound of her friends' voices. She took the stairs two at a time, boots banging off her shins. Setting the boot bag down, she stripped off her work clothes and tossed them in the basket she kept by the bed for laundry. "I'll deal with you later, and you too," she addressed the clothes and the boots.

Twenty minutes later, she gave her still damp hair a quick brush before tying it back in a tail. "I'll find a way to get him alone at some point tonight," she promised herself. Gathering up her dirty laundry, she went downstairs. "Be with you in a sec, I'm just going to put this stuff in the wash," Laurel called into the kitchen as she went through.

"Hallo, Laurel," Aisling greeted her from her place at the head of the small table.

"Hey." Laurel took the chair next to Coll after getting the wash going. He grinned at her and twined his fingers with hers under the table. She leaned into him. "I need to talk to you later," she whispered and straightened in her chair.

"Emily, you have the notes from our last meeting. Have you and the bride added anything?" Sairie inquired.

"Oh a few things." Emily shared a quick smile with Ash.

"Such as?" Coll freed his hand and leaned both elbows on the table. "I'm not wearing some crazy suit with a top hat. You can just forget it." He threw himself back in his seat.

"Neither am I, mate," Gort assured him. "Nothing too fancy."

"No, no. But we did make a couple of small additions to the wedding party," Emily said.

"What do you mean, additions?" Sairie poured tea into their mugs, giving her friend a sidelong glance.

"I asked Stuart to be an usher," Gort blurted, colour rising in his face. "You're the best man, Coll. But Ash and Emily figured we needed at least one usher, and I didn't know who else to ask?"

"Fine by me." Coll shrugged.

"Won't that make the numbers uneven in the wedding party? Or does that matter so much here?" Laurel glanced around the table.

Coll shifted uneasily beside her. Laurel turned, intending to ask him what was bothering him, but was interrupted.

"Hallo, sorry we're late." Stuart come into the kitchen.

Before Laurel could wonder who 'we' was, Lily followed her cousin and pulled up a stool to sit close to Coll.

"Sorry, I had to work late at the shop." She smiled at the room, carefully avoiding Laurel's gaze.

"Lily volunteered to step in as a bridesmaid to even out the numbers," Emily announced.

Laurel clenched her jaw and pasted a stiff smile on her face. "How nice," she managed to say in an almost pleasant voice.

"I talked to Coll about it, and he didn't think anyone would mind. After all, I've been going around with you lot for a while now." Lily finally met Laurel's eyes.

"Of course, no one minds, dear. It was nice of you to offer to even out the numbers," Emily sought to defuse the sudden tension in the room.

The talk of dresses and flowers and guest lists flowed around her. Laurel kept a smile on her face, but her thoughts were far from happy. *Lily talked to Coll about it, did she. And Coll never thought to mention anything to me. Really makes me wonder just how close he's gotten to her lately.*

"What do you think of this dress?" Ash pushed a glossy magazine toward Laurel, the page open to a picture of a dress with a long flowing skirt in a pale green and pink floral design.

"It's beautiful, Ash. Can we order it, or do we have to go up to London to get it? I take it this is the one you've decided on?"

89

"We can order it as long as it doesn't take too long to get here. I didn't order anything yet because I wanted to get your okay. I want a fairy tale kind of wedding, lots of flowers and a big bower covered with flowers for the wedding. Outside, not in the church." Aisling's face clouded for a moment. "Which means that Mum really refuses to attend, not that she was planning to anyway. She says if we don't get married in church we're just living in sin."

Gort reached over and took her hand. "We'll have whatever kind of wedding you want, love. It's your mum's loss if she decides to stay away. Your da has already agreed to give you away, so maybe she'll change her mind."

"It sounds beautiful," Laurel said. "It will be perfect, you wait and see."

"I love that dress. I've loved it from the first time I saw it. I'm so happy you agree with Aisling," Lily gushed.

"Oh, you helped Ash pick out the dress?" Laurel's enthusiasm for the dress waned a bit.

"Actually," Lily looked down for a second, "I saw it in the window of Ezpopsy in London the last time I was up there. I went in and inquired about it, and they were kind enough to give me their catalogue. Ashling loved it as much as I did when she saw it."

"It's a lovely dress and it fits the theme of the wedding perfectly." Laurel avoided Ash who was trying to catch her eye. Suddenly, she felt more than a little like an outsider in her circle of friends.

"Emily and I are planning on a trip up country to Truro or maybe even London to get our outfits. I fancy a fascinator that looks like a scattering of wildflowers, so we'll have to see what we can find. If we do go up to London, we can pick up those dresses." Sairie smiled.

"I thought we'd go next Monday, the crowds won't be as thick as on the weekend," Emily said. "I'm ever so excited about it. I feel like it's my own daughter that's getting married. And Gort, my son, you've been like one of my own your whole life, so I'm torn between being mother of the groom and surrogate mum of the bride." She laughed and hugged Gort, laying a hand on Aisling's arm.

"You can be both," Ash declared, smiling through a sheen of tears.

The talk turned to flowers and if Coll and Gort would build the bower or maybe they should rent one. The wedding was to be held in Sairie's meadow, down by the edge of the small vale. The boys decided they would build it and then Sairie and Emily could use it, if they liked, for their observances of the quarter and cross-quarter days of the eightfold turning of the wheel.

"Oh, I like that idea very much, so I do." Emily clapped her hands. "That's brilliant."

"We'll plant a low hedge with a pretty gateway to keep the ponies from rubbing on it," Sairie decided. "What a perfectly lovely plan. The fuchsia and the hawthorn will be in bloom. Oh, it will be lovely!"

"What about the guest list?" Ash pulled a folded paper out of her satchel. It's not very long, but is there anyone we should add...or take off?"

"Let's see. We'll go over it one more time. We need to get the invites out this week." Emily leaned over so she could share the list in front of Ash. "Your mum and da, Sairie, me, the wedding party of course, we thought maybe Bella and her man if we can contact them, Hamish to perform the ceremony. Did you want to invite any friends from work or from school?"

"I might invite a few girls from work, I'm not sure and you know we're trying to keep the cost down as much as we can. So far that's seven guests plus the seven in the wedding party. Well, it might only be six guests, if Mum doesn't attend. I think that's enough for now."

"How is your dress coming?" Laurel looked across at her friend.

"Oh, it's brill. Emily's altered it to fit me and updated it some so that it's a bit more modern, but it still has that lovely antique feeling. The colour has a sort of patina to it from age, the white is almost a pinky ivory. I just love it. I hope our daughter can wear it one day." Aisling turned her glowing face to Gort.

"You're not preggers, are you?" Lily burst out, hands over her mouth.

"No, I'm not. And don't you go even breathing anything like that around the village," Ash declared.

"Even if she was, it wouldn't matter. Nothing said in this house goes any further, is that understood?" Sairie fixed a dark stare on Lily.

The girl's face went white, and her eyes widened. "No...no...no. I wouldn't..." Lily's voice trailed off and her gaze went to Coll as if seeking reassurance.

"See that you don't. I'll know if you do and you won't like it," Sairie warned her. Then in a quick change of mood, she smiled and stood up. "Anyone want to sample the wedding cakes? I've made three, so you can taste them all and then pick the winner."

Lily stood up, one hand on Coll's shoulder as if to balance herself. "Stuart, we need to get going, I've got the early shift tomorrow..."

"Bloody hell, Lil. There's cake and everything..." He glowered at his cousin.

"Stu...please..."

Muttering under his breath, Stuart got to his feet. "Sorry, I guess we need to take off. If there's chocolate cake, make sure to save me a piece. And my vote goes to anything with chocolate. C'mon, then Lily. Let's go."

"Any flavour of cake you want to put your vote in for?" Emily asked Lily.

"What?" She looked up startled with her hand on the door. "Oh, no. Whatever Aisling and Gort choose is good with me. Night everyone." She hurried out the door.

"Sorry again. I'd really rather stay, but..." Stuart nodded toward the door.

"See you tomorrow at work, mate," Gort called after him.

"Bye," Laurel said, echoed by the others in the room.

"Here we go." Sairie set three plates of cake on the table. "There's a fruit cake, if you want tradition, there's a nice vanilla cream and a lemon. No chocolate, so Stuart's vote doesn't count." Sairie laughed.

After much laughter and a little bit of cake being smeared on faces, the final choice went to Aisling and she chose the vanilla cream, with a request for a small fruit cake just in case her mum thought tradition was important. After all, Aisling's parents had fruit cake at their wedding and kept a bit to celebrate the christening of their first child.

"Ash, do you mind helping Sairie with the clean up? I need to talk to Coll for a moment in private." Laurel sent a pleading look in her friend's direction.

"No need, it will only take a wee minute." Sairie stood and gathered up the tea mugs.

"We'll help," Gort offered. "We have to wait for Coll anyway, he's our ride home."

Laurel got up and turned toward the door, waiting for Coll to follow her. He frowned and shot Gort a puzzled look before he pushed back his chair. Gort gave a one shoulder shrug and transferred a pile of plates onto the counter by the sink.

"Coll?" Laurel opened the door and moved out into the soft twilight gloom.

"What's so bleeding important we can't talk about it in there?" Coll followed her out, his expression more annoyed than puzzled now.

"I think you and I need to talk about some things." Laurel leaned on the side of the house.

"We talk all the time. What's got you all teasy, as Gramma would say?" Coll planted his feet wide and crossed his arms.

"Lily—"

93

"What about Lily?" He stuck his chin out and hunched his shoulders.

"Yes, what about Lily. Is there something going on between you two? Tell me the truth, Coll."

"Going on between us? She's a friend, a good friend."

Laurel snorted. "And that's all? It's certainly not the impression I get when you're both in the same room. The girl can't take her eyes off you and if looks could kill I'd be dead meat. Care to rethink your answer?"

Coll shifted and glanced over Laurel's head toward the pony field. He cleared his throat a couple of times before speaking. "We've hung out a bit, nothing serious. I mean, c'mon Laurel. It's hard when all my mates are going out for drinks or something and I'm the only one who's on his own. Stuart has a girl, and Lily...well Lily works so many hours she hasn't much time for anything else. The few times she has a night off Stuart invites her along and it's only natural that we pair up."

"How convenient." Laurel's lip curled in derision "She's in love with you for heaven's sake. Surely, you're aware of that. You can't be that dense. I mean the way she looks at you ... sickening, if you ask me."

"That's a little harsh, Laurel," Coll ground out the words.

"I don't see you denying it," she challenged him.

Coll shrugged and tipped his head forward.

"How far has it gone then? How much of a fool have I been? Sitting there at the ranch, not going out all that much. Only going out in a group, never just me and a guy. Are you telling me you haven't been on a date with Lily?" Laurel crossed her fingers behind her back.

"Not a real date..." he began.

"I can ask Aisling, she'll tell me the truth if you won't."

"Fine. Yeah, we've been out a few times. To the pictures, dinner a couple of times when she has a night

94

off. Bloody hell, Laurel. It's hard being the only bloke with no girl to go around with. Hard to fit in like."

"I see." Something cold and hard settled in Laurel's stomach. "I guess that tells me what I needed to know." She paused and took a deep breath to ease the tightness in her chest. "I'm done, Coll. We knew from the start this long-distance thing was going to be hard. I was hoping my coming back to Cornwall would solve things, but it hasn't. We've grown up and apart and it's obvious you want more than I'm willing to give you."

"What are you saying?" Coll stared at her in the gathering dusk.

"I'm saying we're through. If you want to go around with Lily, go for it. I've got enough on my plate without Lily staring daggers at me every time she sees me, and me worrying about what's happening when I'm not around. We're through." She wrapped her arms around her waist.

"Laurel... I'm sorry. I never meant for it to happen. And there's always that bloke Chance hanging around you—"

"Don't you dare bring him into this. I have made it very clear to both of you that there is nothing between me and Chance but friendship. He respects that." Fury flared in her eyes and twisted her face. "Don't you ever accuse me of carrying on with Chance. Ever!"

"Sorry, Laurel. I should get going. Early day tomorrow." Coll glanced at his phone.

"Go then. I'll let Gort and Ash know when I go in." She turned on her heel and swept past him, shutting the door with a bit more force than was necessary.

Laurel stood for second in the enclosed porch outside the kitchen door to steady herself. Pushing the door open, she stepped into the yellow light of the kitchen.

"Coll's waiting for you by the car. I can finish with the drying." Laurel took the dish cloth from Gort's hand.

"Is everything okay?" Aisling laid a hand on her arm.

"It is," Laurel assured her. "Now get, you've both got an early morning and so do I." She managed a smile before turning to the drying board by the sink.

"See you tomorrow?" Aisling slipped into her jacket and took Gort's hand.

"After work, for sure." Laurel nodded. "Where do you want to meet?"

"How about a pint at the Admiral Benbow, or maybe Queen's Hotel if you want fancy," Gort suggested.

"What's that other pub, The Turk or something?" Laurel wanted to avoid the Benbow which held memories of better times with Coll.

"The Turk it is. See you around seven?"

"I should be able to make it by then unless Suzy has us working late. Badminton is only a week away and the place is a madhouse."

"Text if you can't make it," Ash said.

"I will." Laurel promised.

The door closed behind them and the sound of Coll's car rolling down the lane came through the window. Sairie plucked the dishcloth from Laurel's hand and pulled her into a chair at the table.

"Now, out with it. What's the trouble? Do I need to wet the tea again?" Sairie squeezed Laurel's shoulder.

"Tea might be good," she agreed.

"Tea solves all problems." Sairie smiled and put the kettle back on the stove.

"There now, tell me what's bothering you." Sairie poured steaming liquid into clean mugs.

Laurel wrapped her hands around the warm crockery to still their trembling. "It's all gone wrong. That's what's wrong. I thought coming here would be a good thing. Give me a chance to spend some time with Coll... and the chance to work with Suzy Wish...I mean what else could I ask for. But nothing is like what I imagined."

"What did you imagine? Are things not working out at the stable yard?"

"No, no. The stable is great. Suzy's great and all the girls. No, it's Coll and me."

"What about Coll and you, lovey?"

"He admitted he's been seeing Lily and going around with her. And it's pretty obvious how she feels about him. It wouldn't be so bad if he'd just told me about it up front, but the fact he's been hiding it makes it feel like it's more serious than I thought."

"What exactly did you think?" Sairie squeezed her hand.

"I thought it was all on Lily's side. That Coll was just being nice to her. I never thought they were going out and about on their own without being in a group. That makes it a date! Like they're a couple."

"I wondered if something like that was happening. Emily was worried about it, and she did speak to me about her concerns, but neither of us had any idea it was anything other than friendship and a convenience to even out the numbers."

Laurel sniffed and wiped the back of her hand under her nose. "Well, it doesn't matter any more. I broke up with him tonight, I think. So he can go chase Lily all he wants."

"I'm sorry, love. Do you want to call your mum and talk it out with her?"

"No. If I tell her, then she'll tell Dad and I'd bet anything that he'll let it slip to Chance. That's the last thing I want. Things are good between Chance and me right now, we can work together and be friends without it being awkward. The minute he feels he might have a shot at something more I'm afraid he'll get ideas about us."

"Would that be so bad? From what you've told me he's turned his life around and is staying clean. It's pretty obvious he has strong feelings for you." Sairie regarded her over the rim of her tea mug.

"I don't know. Maybe that's part of the problem. Until I figure out how I feel about what's happened, I don't even want to think about complicating things anymore than they already are."

"See how things look in the morning, love. Coll will talk to Gort about all this, and he'll tell Aisling who will let you know. It might not be as final as you believe."

"Maybe." Laurel sighed and took mug to the sink. "I'll wash these up and then I'm going to bed. Early morning."

Sairie joined her at the sink, taking the dish cloth from her. "You go on up. I'll take care of this." She gave Laurel a one-armed hug. "Things will look brighter in the morning after a good night's sleep."

"Thanks, Sairie." Laurel left the kitchen and went down the narrow dark hall, trailing her hand along the wall. Up the stairs and in her room, she flopped on the bed staring at the faint shadows on the ceiling.

"If I can sleep at all," she whispered to the silence. Turning on her side she buried her face in the pillow and let the tears come.

* * *

Badminton. Laurel stared wide-eyed out the window of the lorry as it drove up to the stabling area. The scene was like something out of a movie. The landscaped parkland and the imposing stone buildings were so totally different than anything she was familiar with. And the place was huge! She'd be lucky not to get lost between the stables and the rings. She caught sight of some of the cross-country obstacles as the road skirted the course. Her heart skipped. The fences were huge and even she could see how technically difficult they were. Respect for Suzy and Miriam, who would both be tackling that course, rose to new heights.

Once they pulled into the stable area, Laurel was too busy to take any more notice of anything other than settling the horses in their stalls after the vets examined each horse as it arrived. Then Laurel and Fee unpacked the rest of the equipment and stored where Suzy wanted it. She fell into bed exhausted that night at the Devere Totworth Court Hotel. Just wait until she told Carly back in Alberta about this. And she needed to take some pictures on her phone in the morning to send back home. Mom and Dad would love that. She barely heard Fee come in sometime later. She responded to her whispered apology with a mumbled acknowledgement and pulled the pillow over her head.

The next morning, after a breakfast of tea and toast, was spent in lunging the three competition horses, then bathing them before getting them prepared for the first inspection which was to take place in front of Badminton House.

Laurel pulled her attention back to braiding Blue's mane. The big horse stood quietly, and she made sure each braid was identical to its mates. Finally, satisfied with the neat row of braids adorning Blue's arched neck, she tackled the tail braid. Once she was done, she spritzed on some hair spray to hold the ends flat and covered it with a cotton bandage. She finger-combed the long thick hairs below the braid until they fell smooth and lovely down to the straight cut where the hair was banged off evenly. Making sure Blue's coat was shining and immaculate she secured a light stable rug over him before oiling his hooves. Laurel stood back to regard him with a critical eye.

"He looks great, Laurel." Mirima came to stand beside her, already dressed and ready to present Blue to the committee.

"You're sure I haven't missed anything?" Laurel bit her bottom lip.

"Do you have his bridle with you?" Miriam untied the lead rope and glanced at Laurel.

"I'll get it. I have it all polished but kept it in the bag so it wouldn't get dusty or something." Laurel produced the simple snaffle bridle with a regular cavesson noseband that Miriam would use. The silver bit gleamed in the sunlight streaming down.

Miriam ran her hands over the leather and inspected the bit, even checking under the buckles that attached the bit to the headstall. She flashed her groom a grin. "I knew I could count on you, Laurel. Well done." With deft movements she exchanged the head collar for the bridle. Handing the head collar and lead to Laurel, she moved to join the other horses heading toward the front of Badminton House. "Coming?" she called over her shoulder.

"Can I?" Laurel jogged to catch up.

"Yeah. I need you there. Once we're next to go, I need you to strip off the rug and run the stable rubber over him, make sure there's not a speck of dust on him. We'll take off the tail wrap as soon as we get there. Got it?"

"Got it." Laurel could hardly contain her excitement. Her groom credentials prominent on her shirt, her breath came short and it was all she could do to keep up with Blue and Miriam. Forcing herself to take a deep breath, she eased the constriction in her chest. This was so much more than she ever dreamed it would be. The area was full of glossy horses, the murmur of cultured British voices swirling around her. She gave up trying to understand all of the conversations. It seemed the number of different accents was endless, surprising for such a small country compared to Canada. Miriam halted Blue in their assigned order and Laurel make short work of removing the tail wrap, making sure the braid was still tight and flat. She ran her fingers through his long tail, smoothing it as well. Then she waited for Miriam's signal to remove the rug. Suzy and Fee arriving four horse places behind them caught her attention and she gave a small wave to her friend who winked at her, a huge smile on her face.

It was over before Laurel had a chance to get really nervous. She whipped the rug off Blue's back and moved out of the way while Miriam trotted the horse past the committee. She met them at the far end, standing back while they went over the horse.

"That's done, then." Miriam led Blue over to Laurel and handed her the reins. "Put him away please, I have to wait for Suzy and then we have a meeting we need to get to."

"Sure." Laurel slung the rug over Blue, securing it and then leading him back to the stable.

She hadn't done more than get him settled when Fee arrived with Challenger. "Passed with flying colours," she announced. "I don't know why I always get nervous about the inspection, but I do."

"I thought it was just me being new to everything." Laurel laughed.

The two girls settled the horses and then spent some time making sure everything was in order for the next day. Laurel ran a rag over Miriam's dressage saddle, polishing the stirrup irons and then wiping down the already cleaned double bridle. Fee sat next to her doing the same for Suzy's equipment.

"I can't wait to walk the cross-country course. I didn't get to go last year, I had to tag along outside the ropes. Suzy said I get an armband this year." Fee tucked the bridle into its carrier.

"I hope I get to come too. I can't even imagine..."

"You're Miriam's groom, so of course you get to walk it. Lucky git." Fee punched her lightly on the shoulder.

"I'm really worried I'm gonna screw something up. This is nothing like what I've done back home."

Fee laughed. "Don't let all the pomp and posh get to you. Horses are still horses. You'll do fine. Just trust your instincts. I love riding cross-country, but I don't think I'll ever have the nerve to tackle anything like what Suzy and Miriam do. Some of those obstacles...Wow."

"I've looked at the course online, some of them look impossible. I'd have to really, really trust my horse to even point his nose at them."

"I hear you." Fee stood up. "That's everything, let's go get a bite and some tea."

The girls left the tack room, gave the horses one last check, and wandered toward the concession stands.

* * *

Morning came early. Laurel followed Fee to the stables in the pre-dawn gloom. Warm moist air wafted through the trees, the scent of earth, fresh cut grass and the sweet aroma of the hundreds of flowers filling her head.

"This is the easy day. Dressage is usually a long and somewhat boring day." Fee shrugged her jumper closer around her shoulders.

"I really like dressage though. Especially at this level, it's like dancing." Laurel tipped her head back. "Looks like a good day, no clouds."

Fee snorted. "See if you still feel like that after waiting for forever to get your horse in the ring. It's a lot of hurry up and wait." She glanced upward. "And let's hope the day stays clear. You never know."

Five hours later, Laurel could appreciate Fee's opinion. The initial hurry and scurry of getting Blue ready and making sure she had everything she would need for later in her backpack slowed to a snail's pace when Miriam showed up. She was dressed in her white breeches, white shirt, and immaculate stock. She handed Laurel her long boots in their bag, her feet clad in fancy muck boots. Laurel added the bag to her load.

"I've got our order of go. It'll be a few hours before we need to get Blue out. I'm off to watch the first tests and see how the arena is riding." Miriam disappeared into the throng of competitors, owners, and grooms moving toward the dressage ring.

"I just spoke with Suzy. She's in the fourth block of the day, so I've got a long wait." Fee jogged up to the stalls, papers fluttering in her hand.

"When does Miriam go?" Panic flared in Laurel's gut. "She just left and didn't tell me where we are in the order."

Fee smoothed out the papers and consulted them. "Hmmm, oh here it is. Miriam's in the third block, she's...eighth in line."

"How many horses in each block?" Laurel craned her neck to look at the lists.

"Ten. Four blocks of ten today and tomorrow. We're luck we're both today, that means some downtime tomorrow. It's good for the horses too, gives them a bit of a break before the cross-country."

"What do we do now? Can we watch some of the tests?" Laurel glanced toward the stands overflowing with spectators.

Fee consulted her phone. "We should have time. We just need to be back in time to lunge the horses a bit beforehand. And everything, I mean everything, has to be perfect. Not a speck of dust on anything. Suzy goes mental if there's even the tiniest thing wrong."

"Really? She's always so easy going..." Laurel fell into step beside Fee.

"Not at an event, she isn't. You'll see. Be glad you've got Miriam and not Suzy to take care of. Miriam isn't likely to drown you in the lake."

Laurel stopped dead. "Really?"

Fee grabbed her arm and pulled her into motion. "Not really, but she has been known to throw brushes and on one occasion a boot." She shook her head. "That girl didn't last long. And to be fair, she didn't put the breast collar on right and the saddle slipped over a big obstacle and Suzy ended up having to pull up before the next fence."

"Oh." Laurel swallowed hard. "Didn't Suzy check her tack beforehand?"

"Sure, but they depend on us to get it right and keep them and the horse safe. You know how it is when you're on deck at the start box, adrenaline's pumping. It's easy to overlook some tiny thing, that's what we're for. To be sure everything is right, and they come home safe."

"That's true. Abby, my coach at home, did go into that, but we weren't facing anything like these fences. My dad's the same way with things. I guess maybe that's why I'm so careful about checking and rechecking my own tack when I compete."

"That's not a bad thing. But at this level, they really need us to be vigilant on their behalf." She turned to the left and showed her credentials to a security guard before being allowed into an area crowded with other grooms and riders. Laurel followed her.

"You should be able to watch the first block and a few of the second before you need to get back to Blue. Look, here's a good spot." Fee wriggled into a narrow spot and made room for Laurel.

She spent the next two hours watching each horse ride the specified test. The mistakes and miscues were hard to spot, but Laurel was able to appreciate how one ride bested another with judges. The time flew by and before she realized it, it was time to get Blue ready.

Miriam arrived at the stall, just as Laurel finished stowing Blue's wraps in their place. He was saddled underneath a light rug to keep flies and dust away. She ran a soft cloth over his neck and the neat row of braids marching down his arched neck.

"Thanks, Laurel." Miriam took the boot bag she held out to her. In short order she had shed her muckers and stamped into the tall boots.

The light rug slung over her shoulder; Laurel set the mounting block beside the big horse. Miriam swung into the saddle and held her leg out for Laurel to wipe down the boot and the sole of the boot while she pulled on her gloves. Slipping her feet into the stirrups, she nudged Blue into a walk toward the warmup area.

Laurel hurried beside her, excitement swirling in her chest.

She waited at the side with the cluster of other grooms while Miriam took Blue through his paces. When there was only one horse in front of her, Miriam brought him to Laurel and waited while she wiped her boots again and cleaned the foam off the bits and any flecks that marred the horse's chest and shoulders. Laurel gave Blue one last swipe and tapped Miriam's boot for luck before horse and rider moved to await their turn in the ring. Their ride looked almost perfect to Laurel's somewhat prejudiced eye, but Miriam was beaming when she exited the ring.

"Well done." She slapped Blue on the neck and hopped off, handing the reins to Laurel.

"Good trip. It looked great, and Blue was a star." Laurel secured the light rug at his chest.

Miriam laughed. "He does love the crowd. Take good care of our boy, Laurel. See if you can get done in time to watch Suzy's ride. She always wants feedback from us." Miriam undid the long zippers at the back of her tall boots and let Laurel help her pull them off. She took the sneakers Laurel held out to her, slid them on and disappeared into the crowd.

Slinging her backpack over her shoulder, she carried the boots in her hand and led Blue with the other. He was still amped up from his performance, swivelling his head from side to side with a few tiny dancing steps, but following nicely beside her. She passed Fee on her way to the stable going the other way with Challenger.

"How'd it go?" Fee slowed as they passed.

"I thought it looked good. I guess we won't know until we get the scores. He thinks he won the day." Laurel nodded at the preening Blue.

Fee's laugh floated back to her as they moved along.

* * *

"There, that's the last of it." Fee tucked the last bit of tack into its place and stood up.

"I'm done, too." Laurel closed the lid of the trunk and flipped the latch. "I can't wait to walk the course this afternoon. I can't believe some of those fences."

"I'd love to tackle them one day." Fee sighed. "But unless Suzy thinks I'm good enough for one of her horses, I could never afford the calibre of horse to compete at this level."

"It would be awesome, but I'm with you, we couldn't afford a horse like Blue or Challenger. Not to mention Dad would have kittens if he ever saw me point a horse at some of those fences." Laurel giggled.

The two girls left the barn after a last check on their charges. "Suzy's pretty chuffed that both her and Miriam are in the top twenty after the dressage." Fee shook her head. "That's so brill. But it's the cross-country that tells the tale."

"I can't wait until tomorrow." Laurel danced in place. "I'm gonna braid a charm into Blue's mane for good luck. You don't think Miriam will mind, do you?"

"Just make sure it's nothing that will get caught in the reins. And you'd better tell her about it beforehand. Some riders are pretty superstitious. Suzy has a lucky penny she keeps in her left boot. If you watch, you'll see her take that foot out of the stirrup and jiggle it right before she goes into the start box."

"That's kinda cool. I wonder if Miriam has any special ritual she does." Laurel frowned. "I'll have to ask her, just in case I do something to mess it up if I don't know."

"Right. It's just about time. We need to go by the office and pick up the arm bands and a couple more course maps. Suzy's gonna draw all over hers, deciding what line she likes best for what obstacle. We'll get an extra one for Miriam too, just in case she needs it."

Armbands and maps clutched in their hands, Fee and Laurel went in search of Suzy and Miriam. They finally tracked them down in the Pig and Whistle Pub sitting with some of the other riders who rode the day before. The two girls joined them, Laurel sitting back and listening to the riders discussing their test scores as well as some of the cross-country obstacles that were different this year from last year's competition. It took a bit of figuring out all the varied British accents, the woman with the heavy Yorkshire accent had her second guessing some of the terms. Laurel wished she dared record some of the conversation so she could review it later and then see what the difference in the lines they planned to ride would mean once she got out to walk the course.

Laurel left Fee with the others in the pub and wandered over to the dressage ring to watch the last block of ten riders. She was dying to start working on flying lead changes. It was one thing to perform a simple change of leg across a diagonal, or even a few changes with three or four strides in between, but to do two-tempi or one-tempi...her heart skipped a beat as big chestnut crossed the diagonal in one-tempi changes, looking just like he was skipping. She resolved she was going to learn how to ride that movement before she went home to Alberta. Glancing at her watch, Laurel realized it was time to get her butt back to the stalls to meet up with Miriam, Suzy, and Fee. It was also time she was checking on Blue. There might just be time to give him a bit of a lunge before walking the course.

* * *

Laurel squeezed Fee's arm. "I can't believe I'm really here," she whispered. They were walking across the cropped grass of the main arena with the red and white canopies over the spectator boxes marching along the side. She adjusted the armband on her sleeve and hurried to keep up with Miriam who was already walking by the starter fence.

"There you are, Laurel. We'll have to keep moving, the course if four miles long and there are a number of obstacles I'll need to have a good look at. This one is Spiller's Starter and it's pretty straightforward. I'll try to explain things as we go, but there's a few places I want to ask Suzy's advice on."

Laurel trotted after Miriam after taking a long look at the rows of seats and stopping to appreciate the 1.20 metre height of the fence. Fence two was big table jump with a 1.18 metre height and a 2.50 metre spread. She itched to be able to take a shot at jumping it, but knew there was a lot of hard work needed on her part before that could happen.

Miriam and Suzy walked side by side with Fee and Laurel flanking them. Laurel hung on their words, attempting to follow their logic as they discussed the pros and cons of the approaches and lines they planned for each obstacle. Suzy was much more apt to take the direct and often more difficult route where Miriam sometimes chose the less direct route for Blue who wasn't as seasoned as Challenger. As they approached Fence 10A and B Laurel swallowed. She'd have to really trust her horse to take that log jump into the water and then make that sharp right hand turn in the water to jump out again over another log. Suzy and Miriam laughed about getting soaked and hoped it wasn't going to dump rain all over them as well. The Owl Hole, Jump 12A enchanted her. Jump up a steep bank and then through a huge upright circle enclosed with greenery. Now that would be fun, she thought, while realizing the technical accuracy it would involve. The table jumps 18/19AB were set picturesquely with the Badminton House in the background. It was like something out of a fairy tale, Laurel imagined herself riding across the turf and flying over the fences. The combination of obstacles at the Badminton Lake that were jumps 21ABC/22 confused Laurel. There were so many options and she fought to keep the line that Miriam was planning on straight in her head, while Suzy and Fee discussed an alternate more direct route. Fence 23 the Pony Splash looked like great fun and Laurel was pretty sure Blue would love that obstacle. The Voltaire Huntsman Close was another combination that confused Laurel. Too many choices. Suzy remarked how glad she was they'd removed some trees from the area making the route much less fraught with the danger of hitting a tree. Laurel couldn't even imagine trying to figure out a way through the combination while dodging trees as well. Her admiration for Suzy and Miriam as well as the horses went up more than a few notches. She loved the look of the stone walls of the Quarry combination and followed Miriam along the line she planned to take, explaining her thinking to Laurel as they went. As they approached Fence 28, the Brewers Dray, Suzy reminded Miriam to remember not to fly that fence but hold up a bit as it was equipped with mim clips which would cause the fence to come down if you hit it. Then one more fence before entering the main arena again and taking the final fence in front of the stands.

"Don't forget, tomorrow the course will be packed with spectators at every fence and along the way. Don't let Blue get distracted by them," Suzy reminded Miriam. "My first year here, it was me who got overwhelmed by the crowds. I almost missed my line a few times."

"I'm pretty lucky I get kind of tunnel vision once I'm on course, but yeah, this is Badminton, right. I'll keep focussed on the line ahead and ignore the hoards." Miriam took a last look back the way they'd come. The course was dotted with clumps of other competitors studying the fences and the lay of the ground. She clutched the course map in her gloved hand before folding it and tucking it in her pocket. "Bedtime reading." She grinned.

The morning dawned bright and clear, but the forecast did call for showers later in the day. Fee and Laurel were down at the stalls early, making sure everything was in place and the horses were in good order. Both horses didn't have start times until the afternoon. Suzy and Challenger were set to go off at 13:46 and Miriam and Blue at 14:50. Laurel saddled Blue and joined Fee on Challenger. Together they gave the horses a light and relaxing workout, followed by a good grooming. Laurel checked and double-checked Blue's tack, testing the stirrup leathers even though she knew they were almost new. She polished and repolished the silver buckles and the stirrup irons, along with Miriam's spurs. The bridle hung ready on its hook, but she wiped the bit again with a soft cloth. Miriam's boots gleamed in the dim light of the stable. Laurel made sure she had her groom's credentials in full view. Miriam's bib with her competitor number hung with her protective vest and helmet. Even though Laurel was certain everything was in place, she couldn't keep still. She fussed with Blue's mane and tail, grooming his sleek coat one more time. She took the tiny silver charm she'd gotten Miriam's permission to braid into the hair at top of his poll and secured it firmly in place.

"There now, buddy. You've got extra protection. That'll bring you both home safe and sound. Be careful out there and jump well." Laurel kissed his nose and went to see if Fee needed anything since Suzy was set to go off first.

* * *

Before it seemed possible, Laurel was giving Miriam a leg up onto Blue and running a cloth over his neck and wiping the bit one last time.

"Thanks Laurel." Miriam's mouth twisted in a tense smile. "We're next. Be sure to be there to meet me after the finish."

"Have a good trip," Laurel called as Blue danced away. She moved out of the way and watched Blue leave the start box and gallop up the grass in the arena to the first fence which he sailed over and then disappeared through the alleyway under the tented stands, headed toward the second fence. Gathering her equipment, Laurel moved to where she could watch the large screens situated around the area and follow Blue's progress around the course. She saw that Suzy and Challenger had come through unscathed, Suzy must be somewhere watching and Fee would be back in the stable area taking care of Challenger. Laurel turned her attention back to the screens, glad she didn't have to go far as the last obstacle was placed in the main arena as well as the start fence. Blue was approaching the Badminton Lake combination and Laurel held her breath. This was the one that Miriam was wary of for some reason. The big grey took the straighter route over the big corner of 21AB and headed for 21C where Miriam collected him a bit and they took the fence with a big drop into the water. Laurel held her breath at the big splash but Blue surged ahead and took the big upright brush fence out of the water and back into it. So far so good, they just had the big bank out of the lake to negotiate.

Everything looked good, Blue's ears were pricked forward, and Miriam seemed to have things well in hand. Laurel let her breath out and then caught it again. Blue hesitated coming into the bank, maybe the huge crowd distracted him, but his hind end slipped as he tried to gain footing and then after what seemed like forever, his haunches went from under him, and he landed heavily on his side. Laurel gasped, and in a panic couldn't decide what she was supposed to do. She looked for an official to ask if she should try and get to the lake or if she should wait, or should she find Suzy...or Fee... Her gaze was fixed on the screen where Blue thrashed in the lake. *Where is Miriam? Oh God, don't let her still be under him?* Her phone vibrated in her pocket, and she yanked it out. It was Fee telling her to come back to the stables and wait for Blue and Miriam there. Shoving the phone back in her pocket she raced through the crowd as fast as she could, arriving sweating and dishevelled at the stalls where Fee was pacing back and forth. Challenger stood blanketed in his stall, cooling off after his bath.

"What happened? Are they okay?" Laurel gasped out the words.

"I think so, I don't know. Suzy's talking to the officials at the fence, she's on her way out there. They've held the horses behind them until they can get Blue and Miriam clear."

"They have to be okay. They have to be." Laurel paced with Fee. "Is there anything we should be doing to get ready for them to come back?"

"We won't really know what's needed until we get some kind of report on what the damage is, if any." Fee tried to sound positive, but her voice wavered.

After what seemed like an age, Fee's phone binged. She whipped it out of her vest. "Okay, Blue's in the horse ambulance on his way back here, Miriam's on her way to the hospital. Maybe a broken arm or shoulder."

"What about Blue?" Laurel peered at the screen. "Why does he need transport?"

"No idea, but it might just be that the transport is quicker to get him off the course than leading him back. Suzy's with him, so she'll make sure he's getting the best of care."

Fee swallowed hard and gripped Laurel's hand. "It's gonna be okay, it's gonna be okay," she kept repeating. Laurel gripped her hand back and bit her lip.

Moments later, the ambulance halted at the end of the row and Suzy jumped out. Laurel and Fee ran to join her, Laurel flinging the cooler over her shoulder, head collar and shank in her hands. She skidded to a stop ahead of Fee, putting a hand on the lorry to steady herself.

"Is he okay? Did he hurt anything?" Her eyes sought Suzy's, trying to judge by her expression how bad things were.

"Nothing too serious. We'll know more once the vet has a chance to examine him better. For now, it looks like he's hurt his left foreleg, he's putting weight on it, but not much. Other than that, it's hard to tell. Maybe strained his shoulder, and they'll have to assess his back and hind end. It looked like he landed pretty heavy on his left side. Got his foreleg caught in the reins somehow." Suzy turned to help the attendants get Blue out of the trailer.

"Hey buddy." Laurel moved to his head and stripped off the bridle with the broken reins while slipping the head collar on. Fee took the sodden bridle from her, pulled the cooler off Laurel's shoulder and threw it over the horse's back. Suzy was bent down with the vet looking at Blue's foreleg which he held with just the toe sitting on the ground.

"Hold him still as you can," Suzy told Laurel. "Keep him calm. They're bringing the portable x-ray."

Laurel stood by Blue's head, stroking his shoulder and murmuring to him. Fee flipped the cooler back long enough to remove the saddle, breast collar and pad, then covered him again. "Thanks, Fee," Laurel called while Fee hauled the dripping gear into the tack room. "I'll take care of that once we get Blue settled."

"No worries, Laurel. I'll get the brush boots off him too."

"I can get this one." Laurel bent and carefully removed the protective covering on the injured leg. "Good man." She stroked his shoulder while the horse stood quietly.

"Miriam's fine. I just spoke with the hospital. She's got a dislocated shoulder and a broken arm. They're deciding if they need surgery to pin the bone or if it will heal on its own. But the good news is, she's going to be just fine." Suzy came back with the vet and his technician who was carrying the portable x-ray. "Now let's see what's up with this boy."

Laurel stepped back out of the way, holding Blue's head steady.

113

* * *

Later, after settling Blue in his stall and cleaning his tack, Laurel wended her way back to the room she shared with Fee. Finding it empty, she piled up some pillows and took out her phone. She texted Coll and waited for him to reply. Things had been a bit better after the blowup. Coll had apologized and promised it was Laurel he wanted to be with and not Lily. Laurel believed he was sincere and agreed to give their relationship another chance. After ten minutes she gave up and texted Aisling telling her about the accident and asking if she'd seen Coll lately. Aisling's reply came quickly expressing concern for Blue and Miriam. She, however, avoided mentioning Coll. Biting her lip, Laurel debated pushing the issue and asking about Coll again. Her pride got the upper hand and she texted Ash that she'd see her soon.

Laurel stared at the phone for a long moment and then texted Carly and Chance. She hadn't talked to either of them in over a week. Well, probable closer to a month since she'd contacted Chance. She hit send and then grinned, Carly was probably at work and not able to respond yet and Chance...well he might be anywhere and maybe out of cell range. Tossing the phone on the bed, she headed into the bath where she stripped off her clothes and stood under the shower letting the hot water ease the tension in her muscles. She lingered under the spray until the skin on her fingers puckered. Sighing, she dried off and got dressed. Glancing at the clock on the side table, she was surprised to see it was eight-thirty. Time to go check on Blue. Retrieving her phone from the folds of the bedspread she noted the message icon indicated someone had replied.

"Of course, it was Chance." A reluctant grin spread across her face. "Somehow I can always count on him to be there." She flicked the screen and read the text. He was complaining about Carly and Joey spending too much time together again and only near the end did he comment on Blue and hoped that the horse would recover. He signed it with a C and oxo which she could have done without. Still no reply from Coll. She sighed. Well, maybe he was working late or something. Or so she convinced herself for the moment.

"Hey!" Fee opened the door just as Laurel was reaching for the handle.

"Hey yourself," she said, stepping back to let Fee enter. "I'm just headed back to check on Blue. You look pretty pleased with yourself." Laurel smiled.

"Yeah, been celebrating a bit. Challenger and Suzy are in the top five after the cross country." A huge smile split Fee's face. "Isn't that incredible?"

"Wow! That's awesome! I forgot to even ask how they ended up I was so worried about Blue."

"How's he doing?" Fee flopped on the bed, grinning sillily at the ceiling.

"Vet said nothing too serious, a bad strain. They already did a laser treatment and he's got some meds he needs to take. I've got it all written down." Laurel paused by the door. "Do you want me to give Challenger his night hay and check on him while I'm there?"

Fee rolled over onto her side. "Would you mind? Suzy was in a great mood, and I think I celebrated a bit too hard."

"Suzy wasn't celebrating as hard as you, was she?" Laurel quashed a surge of concern.

"No." Fee shook her head. "Nope, she's all professional that girl. Had one glass of wine and that was it." She grinned. "I made up for her abstinence though."

"I guess. At least you don't have to ride tomorrow, just get Challenger ready for the stadium jumping."

"You got that right." Fee yawned. "Morning comes early. Thanks for looking after Challenger tonight. I owe you one."

"No worries. I'm going over to the hospital in the morning to see Miriam after I take care of Blue, but I should be back in time to help you with Challenger if you want."

"Sure, always good to have another pair of hands. If the weather does what it's supposed to, we might need to put the mud calks in. Suzy'll decide once she gets a look at the footing in the morning."

Laurel closed the door and made her way to the stables. Her phone vibrated and she yanked it out of her pocket. To her disappointment it wasn't Coll, but Carly full of news about Joey and her job and a bit about Chance and what he was up to, which was more than Chance himself had shared with her. Laurel texted a quick reply before collecting what she needed for Blue.

The big grey seemed comfortable enough, moving a little in his straw and eager for his night hay. She mixed his medication with a bit of molasses and then let him lick her fingers clean. After checking his water bucket was full, his leg wraps were in good order and straightening his stable rug, she left him happily eating and went to do the same for Challenger.

"You've got a big day tomorrow, you." She smoothed his forelock and ran a hand down his neck. Laurel adjusted his rug which had shifted a bit and checked his water before giving him his night rations. "You be a good boy, jump well for Suzy, okay?" Laurel gave him a hug before securing the door of his stall. "See you two in the morning. Don't do anything I wouldn't do." She giggled as she headed back to the hotel.

Chapter Ten

Laurel squealed with delight and found herself engulfed in Fee's hug. Challenger and Suzy cleared the last fence and dashed between the timers. A clear round with no time faults put her in second place with only one horse left to jump.

"Oh my God, the worst we can do is third place." Fee danced in place and then rushed to Challenger's side. "Way to go, Suzy!"

Suzy allowed herself a grin and slid off her horse before moving to watch the last rider negotiate the course. Laurel took the reins from Fee.

"Go on and watch. I've got him." Laurel threw a light rug over the big horse's back and led him into the hitching ring to wait for the results. She craned her neck but couldn't see more than one of the jumps in the ring. "Ye-s-s-s-s." The word hissed between her teeth when a loud groan rose from the stands. A rail down meant four faults and ensured that Suzy maintained her grip on second place in the stadium jumping. Laurel had no idea what that meant in terms of the final placings for the event but figured it sure couldn't hurt.

"Here, I'll take him now." Fee came jogging up to her.

Laurel whipped the rug off Challenger and handed Fee the reins. She followed behind the pair, not wanting to miss Suzy's victory lap behind the winner. Her heart thrilled as the horses galloped around the outside of the ring, the soaring notes of music from the band almost drowned out by the roar of the crowd. Laurel hugged herself. This was so much better than anything she ever imagined. Every fibre of her body wanted to be out there. Maybe, maybe before the summer was out, Suzy would make good on her promise and let Laurel compete in a local event.

* * *

The trip home was made on a celebratory note. Suzy and Challenger had finished fifth overall and Blue was going to recover fully. Laurel sat back and listened to Suzy and Fee hash over the cross-country trip and where a quicker or different line might have been a better choice. Miriam leaned against the back of the seat beside Laurel, eyes closed, cradling her arm which was encased in plaster.

"You okay?" Laurel whispered.

Miriam opened her eyes a crack. "Yeah, the pain meds make me sleepy, but the arm isn't feeling too bad right now." Her eyes drifted closed again.

Laurel checked the camera app on her phone that showed her the horses in the float behind them. Challenger was tossing hay out his hay net while Blue was resting his nose on the chest guard, eyes half-closed. The bit of tranquilizer the vet had administered to keep him quiet and steady for the ride home seemed to be doing the trick. Laurel turned her attention back to the conversation between Fee and Suzy, eager to glean every bit of information from it she could.

The lorry and float bumped up the lane of Longrock Equestrian causing Miriam to straighten in her seat.

"We're home." Laurel patted her knee. "You get on home, I'll take care of everything here. You look beat."

Miriam yawned and then grimaced when she moved her injured arm. "Are you sure? I know I'm not much help, but I hate to dump everything on you."

"Forget it. You go home and rest. Blue and I will be just fine. And the stable crew will be there to pick up the slack if need be," Laurel assured her.

Miriam didn't look convinced. But the moment she stepped out of the lorry, Suzy descended on her and arranged for one of the stable staff to drive Miriam to her flat. Laurel watched the small car bump out of sight and then hurried to carefully manoeuvre Blue off the horse float. He was walking a bit better and putting more weight into his leg, but Laurel was anxious he didn't over do it. His stall was almost knee deep in straw when she reached it. She slid off the head collar, made sure the water was fresh and that his hay net was placed where he didn't need to move much to access it. By the time Laurel had removed the shipping bandages, replaced them with stable wraps and changed the bandages supporting his blown tendon the horse float was already unloaded. Challenger stuck his head over his stall guard as she passed, sprigs of hay sticking out his mouth. Laurel ran a hand down his neck before joining Fee in the tack room where she was storing the equipment.

"Good to be home." Fee glanced up with a grin.

"It is. I wouldn't have missed Badminton for the world." Laurel paused. "Although I would have preferred it if Blue and Miriam didn't have a wreck."

Fee shrugged. "It's all part of the game. It's weird, though, to hear someone saying there was fence down on the cross-country. That's new and it's gonna take some getting used to."

"Yeah, I guess. But those mim clips will save a lot of horses from getting hurt I bet." Laurel pulled a load of leg wraps out of the washer and tossed them into the dryer.

"That's what they say. I know some of the traditionalists think it's gonna dilute the calibre of horse and rider. Takes some of the danger out of it. Like any change there's always gonna be some who resist, but the organizers and especially the sponsors want to ensure the public that every precaution to protect the horses is being taken. Bad press because a horse or rider is badly hurt or gets killed is the last thing they want."

"It's the same back home with the rodeo and the chuck wagon races, but no matter what precautions you take accidents are still going to happen." Laurel picked up her duffle bag and surveyed the room. "I think that's everything, right?"

Fee glanced at the still whirring dryer. "We can take care of those in the morning..."

"What are you two still doing here?" Suzy stood in the doorway of the tack room. "Go on, get out of here. Whatever isn't done can wait 'til morning as long as the horses are settled."

"Horse are taken care of, Suzy," Fee said.

"Then go home. I'm for a huge glass of wine and bed." She disappeared and then stuck her head back in the door. "Top five, who would have guessed." A brilliant smile shone on her face before she disappeared again.

"See you in the morning." Laurel slung her duffle bag over her shoulder and went in search of her bicycle. She could call Sairie to come and get her; and given the complaint of her muscles as she swung a leg over her bike, the idea had merit. But the solitary ride along the narrow Cornish lanes would give her the time to relive the highlights of the last six or seven days. She pushed the images of Blue and Fee floundering in the lake from her mind and concentrated on their dressage test and Suzy's success. Laurel was astounded at how much she'd learned just from being around a competition of that calibre. More than anything she wanted to be out there up on a good horse riding at one of the imposing obstacles. Dad would have kittens, but she thought her mom would understand. Dad was always cautioning her to rein in her competitiveness, not to take reckless chances when she ran the barrels or the few times he came to watch her compete in the jumper ring. Maybe some day she'd compete in the International Ring at Spruce Meadows. She frowned when her front tire hit a bump and almost unseated her duffle bag. For really competitive three day or combined training events though, she'd have to either go east to Ontario or Quebec or into the States. Laurel shook her head. There was no way Dad would be okay with that. "Cross that bridge when I come to it," she said, turning into Sairie's lane.

"I'm home!" Laurel caroled pushing open the inner door into the kitchen.

"How was Badminton? Everything you thought it would be?" Sairie got up to put the kettle on. "Are you hungry, then?"

"Badminton was amazing! I can't even begin to tell you." She dropped into a chair at the table. "I'm starving. We stopped to grab some takeout for lunch, but that was hours ago."

Sairie busied herself constructing a sandwich while waiting for the kettle to boil. "I saw on the telly there were a few wrecks at some of the fences. Anyone get hurt that you knew?"

"Yeah. Blue and Miriam had a wreck at the lake. They got through the combination, but Blue slipped coming up the bank and fell on Miriam."

"My stars! Are they both okay?" Sairie turned, mustard pot in her hand.

"Sort of. Miriam has a broken arm and Blue hurt his leg. But they should both recover fully according to the doctors. Scared the crap out of me, though. I saw it happen on the big screen by the start. I just wanted to start running, but it was a long way, and Fee told me to get my ass back to the stall and wait for the horse ambulance to bring Blue. Suzy went to make sure Miriam was taken care of."

"Well, it sounds like everything will be fine in the end." Sairie put a sandwich and crisps on the table in front of Laurel. "Eat up."

"Thanks." Laurel dug into the food. By the time the tea was ready the plate was empty. "Ta," she said when Sairie placed a steaming mug in front of her. "Tell me what's been going on here while I've been gone. I texted with Ash a bit, but it was pretty busy and she's fussing about the wedding."

"Did you have much chance to speak with Coll?" Sairie regarded her over the rim of her mug.

"Not really. Why?" Doubt and suspicion reared its head. "I did text him a few times, but it took forever for him to reply and then it was only one-word answers." Laurel took a sip of tea and steeled herself to voice her suspicion. "Has he been hanging out with Lily while I've been gone?"

"I wouldn't say that so much...she's been helping out with the preparations for the reception, so I'm sure she and Coll have seen each other, but other than that I can't say. It's something you should discuss with Coll."

"Hmmm." Laurel frowned at Sairie. "That's your story and you're sticking to it?"

"If you like." Sairie grinned. "Far be it from me to get in the middle of a lovers spat."

"Lovers, ha!" Laurel snorted and pushed her plate away. "I'll just wash these up and then I'm for bed. Tomorrow is another day and I need to look after Blue's leg first thing, so I need to get in early."

"You run along. I'll take care of the washing up." Sairie dropped a kiss on Laurel's head. "You should either text or ring your mum and dad, they'll have followed the event online and maybe they've figured out that one of your lot was involved in a crash. They must be worried. When was the last time you talked to them?"

"Oh! Not since yesterday." Laurel pulled out her phone and slid her finger up the screen. The screen remained dark. "Oh, dammit, I forgot to charge it. I've been so busy with Miriam and Blue and helping pack up for the trip home I must have forgotten."

"Maybe there's a message from Coll that you've missed then," Sairie suggested.

"Yeah, maybe." Laurel doubted that was the case but refrained from saying anything. "I'll go plug it in up in my room and text Ash, let her know I'm back."

"Text Coll too, lovey," Sairie prodded her.

"Yeah, maybe. I'll think about it."

"If I was a betting woman, I'd bet there's a text from him." A tiny smile lifted the corner of Sairie's mouth.

"We'll see. I'll let you know if you're right in the morning." Laurel grabbed her duffle bag and left the kitchen into the narrow dark hallway, running her fingers along the wall until she reached the steep stairs. After a quick wash up, she pushed open the door of her room and collapsed on the bed. Taking a moment to rummage in her bag she pulled out her charger cord and plugged her phone in. She stared at it for a long moment and then set it on the dresser. If there was a message from Coll it would still be there in the morning and if there wasn't...well whether she looked at it now or in the morning that wouldn't change either. A huge yawn made something crack in her jaw. Aisling could wait until morning too. Laurel lay back on the quilt and closed her eyes.

* * *

"I can't believe the wedding is tomorrow." Laurel turned from the mirror where she'd been critically regarding her reflection. "You're sure this dress looks okay? I mean, it's pretty and all, but are you sure it shouldn't be let out a bit?" She twisted to look at the back. "Or taken in a bit?" She tugged at the flowing skirt.

"Laurel, you look lovely. The dress is fine. Honestly, you'd think you were the bride and not me." Aisling laughed and handed Laurel the tiny floral fascinator. "Here, try this on with the dress. Let me see if it looks like I thought it would."

Laurel took the arrangement of cream and pink flowers mixed with sprays of some white frothy things and regarded it with skepticism. "You think this will actually stay on?"

"It will. Go ahead, try it on." Aisling stood next to her, so the two girls were reflected in the mirror.

Laurel fitted the tiny combs into her hair and then held her hands on either side, ready to catch it in case it came adrift.

"Oh my! It's perfect." Tears sparkled in Aisling's eyes. "Tomorrow the hairdresser will fix it so it won't move no matter how windy it might get. Coll won't be able to take his eyes off you." Ash hugged Laurel.

"Careful." Laurel laughed as the fascinator tipped forward over her forehead. She extracted it from her long hair and set it carefully on the dresser. "I'm glad you went with silk flowers, I was worried about the real flowers wilting if the sun was too hot tomorrow. Sairie says the weather is going to be perfect."

"It better be. I only plan on getting married once." Ash fake scowled at the window where the sun was burnishing everything in gold and orange. "Red sky at night, sailor's delight."

"Has your mom changed her mind?" Laurel slipped out of the dress and tucked it into the zippered bag hanging on the back of the door.

"No. And I don't suppose she will either." Aisling sighed. "Dad is coming to give me away in spite of Mum going on and on about what a disaster my marriage will be."

"I'm sorry, Ash. What are the boys up to tonight?" Laurel changed the subject, hoping to make her friend smile.

"Lord only knows. Coll and Stuart are taking Gort out for one last bachelor blast." She giggled. "I can't imagine. Gort never touches the drink, you know...after Daniel...so lets hope Coll isn't green in the morning. Stuart is only the usher so if he has to dash into the shrubbery to sick up it won't matter as much."

"Hopefully Coll will have enough sense to not get too wrecked." Laurel frowned. "What's Lily up to tonight? Not shadowing the boys, is she?"

Aisling shrugged. "I'm not sure. I put her in charge of arranging everything for the reception. You know, the tablecloths, centre pieces, serving dishes. I'm sure Sairie has her well in hand." She paused and regarded her friend, a serious expression on her pretty face. "You shouldn't worry about Lily, you know. Coll is mad over you, anyone can see that. Have you two spent much time together lately?"

"Some. He's been so busy with Gort's side of the wedding planning and between work and helping you we just haven't had a lot of time to talk."

Aisling gripped her hand. "It'll all work out. You'll see. Coll is just being nice. You know Lily's never had many friends and well...I think he feels sorry for her. It's you he can't take his eyes off."

"It's been hard, though. This long-distance thing is difficult and I was hoping that coming here would help. But I'm not sure it is. " She sat on the edge of the bed. "But enough of that. Are you ready for tomorrow? No last minute jitters? No second thoughts?"

Aisling perched beside her. "Not a one. This is what I've wanted for so long I can't believe it's actually happening."

"Sairie and Emily have your dress all pressed and ready. Coll will bring the flowers in the morning. I can't wait to see your bouquet, and mine. We'll have to make sure we get the right corsages to the right people. I love the one you picked for Emily."

"Gort picked that one. Emily's been like a mother to him, and he wanted her to have something really special. She loves lilies and roses, but I think those tiny orchids and the little pink and cream rosebuds will please her."

"I think so too. I'm so glad you're staying here tonight."

"Me too. I'm so excited I don't think I'll be able to sleep anyway, so this is perfect." Aisling moved to lean against the pillows piled at the headboard.

"You'll have to try, though. Can't have the bride walking down the aisle with bags under her eyes." Laurel joined her at the head of the bed.

"Heavens no." Aisling laughed. "Or, God forbid, I fall asleep at the altar."

"Not much chance of that."

"I suppose not."

They lapsed into silence. Laurel caught her head bobbing down waking her from a drowse. Aisling was curled at her side, head resting on Laurel's shoulder, fast asleep. She slid them both down into a more comfortable position and pulled a knitted blanket up over them. "Happy dreams," she whispered and closed her eyes.

* * *

The morning passed in a blur of motion. Laurel wolfed down a piece of toast while pacing Sairie's kitchen and making sure Aisling ate some breakfast. Sairie swept in and out of the cottage, arms full of ribbons and Lord knew what else.

"Do you need any help with the bower?" Laurel tossed the last crust of toast into the bucket where they kept the scraps for the chickens.

Sairie stopped in mid-stride. "Whyn't you come along and see what you think of what I've managed so far?" She bustled out the door.

Laurel followed, trailed by Aisling, out into the yard where the grass was clipped close, and a flower and ribbon bedecked bower stood guarded by some tall Leyland Cypress trees. The tent where the reception would take place was set off to the side and it was here that Sairie headed.

"Come along," she called over her shoulder, "I could use your help setting the centrepieces and arranging the other flowers."

"Sairie, it's magic, like a fairyland in here." Laurel stopped in the entryway. Early morning sunlight glowed through the canvas illuminating the space with a golden blush of colour. The tables were covered with floral tablecloths in pastel hues, tall candles in brass holders sat on each table waiting for the finishing touches.

"It's better than I ever imagined," Aisling's voice broke on the words, tears glimmering in her eyes. "How can I ever thank you?"

Sairie set her bundle down on a convenient chair and enfolded Ash in her arms. "It's my pleasure to do this for you and Gort. The best gift you can give me is for you and Gort to live a long happy life together." She kissed Ash's forehead and released her. "Now, let's get these things in place. Time waits for no one."

Quicker than Laurel would have thought possible the bounty of flowers and ribbons were in place, a light breeze wafting through the open doors of the tent setting the ribbons and streamers dancing.

Aisling clapped her hands. "Oh my, they look like I feel. Like they can't wait for everyone to be in here and celebrating."

"First, lovey, we need to get you cleaned up and into your wedding dress before anyone decides to show up early."

The three women left the tent and after inspecting the arbour one last time, they made their way back to the cottage.

"Have you heard from Emily?" Laurel whispered to Sairie. "How are things going there?"

"As well as can be expected, I suppose. Gort is shaking with nerves, and it didn't help that Alice showed up at the door in tears begging the poor child not to marry her daughter and destroy her life."

"Oh no! How could her mom do that? Today of all days." Laurel glanced toward Aisling who was already at the back door. "Ash doesn't know about this, does she?"

"My stars, no. And she won't unless Gort decides to tell her after the wedding."

"You don't think Alice'll show up here, do you? Try to stop the ceremony?" Laurel glanced at Sairie in horror while waving at Ash who was waiting impatiently by the door.

"Tom will make sure she stays away," Sairie assured her.

"But Ash's dad is going to be here to give her away. How is he supposed to keep her mom from coming?" Laurel worried her bottom lip with her teeth.

"I've left that up to Tom, but he is very definite that Alice will not ruin Aisling's special day. Now come along, the bride is waiting, and if we linger here much longer, she's going to figure out something's up."

Sooner than Laurel expected the crunch of tires on laneway announced the arrival of someone who was far too early.

"Who can that be?" She craned her neck to look out her bedroom window. "It's way too soon for any guests to get here, isn't it?"

"God, I hope it's not guests. I'm not near ready." Aisling swivelled on the stool by the mirror, mascara brush in hand.

"Well, whoever it is can just wait until we're ready. Sairie will head them off." Laurel turned back from the window. She opened the bedroom door and stuck her head out into the hall. "Sairie! Someone's here."

"I've got it in hand," the older woman's voice echoed up the narrow stairwell.

Laurel shut the door and wandered back to the window. "Oh, it's Stuart. He must have come over early in case we needed help with something...oh for the love of God!" She spat the last words in disgust.

"What is it?" Aisling left the mirror and joined Laurel at the window.

"Lily. I just wish she wasn't part of the wedding. That's horrible of me, isn't it?" Frustration roiled in Laurel's gut.

"Sairie did ask her to help with some of the arrangements and she is my lone brides maid to even up the numbers." Aisling laid a hand on her friend's arm. "I'm sure she's just trying to be helpful."

"Look at her dress," Laurel wailed. "She looks better than I do in it, and I hate that she chose it." Laurel whirled away from the window.

Aisling peered out clad in her bridal lingerie, careful to stay out of the line of sight of anyone looking up. Lily passed below, the skirts of her long flowing dress rippling in the light breeze, high heels sinking in the grass. "Well, I love the dress too, don't forget. And you look brilliant in it, it suits your colouring far better than Lily." Aisling turned back into the room. "Let's not let this ruin our day, Laurel."

"You're right. This is your day, and nothing is going to ruin it, let alone someone like Lily, or me being catty." Laurel thrust her frustration and annoyance aside and turned her attention to helping Aisling with her hair.

"Oh my, don't you look a sight." Sairie stopped in the doorway of Laurel's room to admire Aisling. "You look a treat, lovey. It's almost time. Do you girls need my help with anything? Emma is downstairs waiting to put the finishing touches on your hair and pin Aisling's veil in place and Laurel's fascinator."

"I can't believe it's actually time. I feel like I've been waiting for this my whole life." Aisling pressed both her hands to her heart. "Look at me, I'm shaking." She laughed, holding out her hands. "Is Da here yet?"

"Tom's downstairs, he came along with Stuart." Sairie unzipped the covering of Aisling's dress. "Ready?"

"Oh yes." Aisling waited for Sairie and Laurel to release the dress from the plastic and then stepped into the folds and let her two attendants ease the fabric up over her hip, slipping her arms into the sleeves and turning for them to fasten the back for her. She smoothed the silken fabric with her palms, admiring the slight sheen and glints picked out the sunlight through the window. "It's perfect, isn't it?" Aisling turned her watery gaze to Laurel.

"It is. No one is going to even notice anyone else once they see you. Poor Gort might just faint plain away."

"Oh I hope not." Aisling giggled.

"You let Coll worry about the groom." Sairie grinned. "Now let's get you and that dress downstairs so Emma can fasten your veil. Laurel, do you need any help with your gown?"

"Nope, I'm good. You go take care of the bride." Laurel grinned. "I'll be down in just a minute." She waited until the rustle of skirts and Aisling's giggles faded before she unzipped her own dress from its bag. It was as pretty as she remembered. Prettier, and more expensive, than any dress she'd ever owned. Holding it up, she eyed the skirt. Perhaps, it could be shortened afterward so she could wear it again. But that was for later. For now she needed to get into it without smudging her makeup.

Minutes later she made her way carefully down the narrow stairs and into the kitchen. It seemed everything centred around Sairie's kitchen.

"How do I look? Is the back done up right?" Laurel turned on her toes, the long skirts swishing around her ankles.

"You look amazing," Aisling declared.

"Here let me fix this." Sairie held Laurel still while she adjusted the hook and button at the back of her waist. "There now. Just sit you down here and Emma will take care of you once she's got the bride all set."

Laurel perched on the edge of a chair not wanting to get any creases in her dress. Aisling was positively glowing, sitting in a ray of sunlight, her blue eyes bright with happiness and nerves. Laurel envied the aura of joy surrounding her friend and the almost visible assurance that she was making the best and most important decision of her life. There could be no doubt looking at her that Aisling had found the love of her life. If only Laurel could be as sure of her feelings for Coll, things would be much less complicated. Just to further muddy the waters of her emotions, Chance texted in the middle of night to wish her luck with the wedding preparations. She shook her head to rid it of the distracting thoughts. Today the only thing that mattered was making sure Aisling and Gort had the perfect day. Lily and Coll, and Chance be damned.

"Your turn." Aisling got up carefully and went to examine her reflection in the mirror by the sink.

Laurel sat and permitted herself to be prodded and poked by the hairpins and combs until Emma proclaimed that nothing short of high gale would remove the fascinator from Laurel's hair. Rising, she joined Ash by the mirror. Her long, normally straight blond hair was twisted and tortured into an up do and sitting atop it was the silly frothy excuse for a hat. Turning her head, she had to admit the affect was actually quite pretty. Her thoughts strayed for a second, Chance would laugh his ass off if he ever saw her like this. Pushing the thought away, she turned her back on the mirror.

"Are the boys here yet?" Laurel peered out the side window.

"I see Coll's car out there, so I think it's safe to say the groom has arrived safely." Sairie's mouth tilted in a wry grin.

"Look at you!" Emily sailed in the door, pretty in her pale lavender dress. "Oh, my. I'm so happy for you." She kissed Aisling on both cheeks, mindful of her hair and make up. Stepping back, she gestured toward the door. "And look who I found!"

"Mom! Daddy!" Laurel threw herself into her parents' arms. "What are you dong here? I thought you said you couldn't make it?"

"Your mom insisted we get ourselves here and Chance is holding down the fort at home." Colt Rowan extracted himself from his daughter's embrace. "I can't believe I'm looking at my little girl. When did you go and grow up on me?"

"Colt!" Anna Rowan slapped her husband playfully on the arm. "She's been grown up for a while, you've just ignored the fact."

"Wow, just wow." He stood back and gazed at his daughter. "I need a picture of this." He whipped out his phone and captured Laurel and her mother laughing with their arms around each other.

"Where are you staying? When did you get here? I still can't believe you're here," Laurel couldn't get the words out fast enough.

"Emily has been kind enough to offer us a room and we got in late yesterday. Too late to even think about calling you." Anna hugged her daughter.

"Thank you for coming." Aisling gave Anna a hug and smiled at Colt. "Gort will be thrilled to see you and so will Coll."

"Hmmm, yes, Coll." Colt winked at Laurel. "I'll have to keep my eye on that young man with my daughter looking like she does in that dress."

"Daddy!" Heat rose up Laurel's throat.

"Come along now." Emily herded them toward the door. "It's time to take our places. The groom is waiting for us. Tom is right outside the door, and once Stuart shows us to our seats, he'll bring Aisling along. Wait for the music, mind." She disappeared out the door behind Laurel's parents and Sairie in a flash of lavender.

"Ready?" Laurel took Aisling's hands.

"Yes. Oh, yes."

"Don't Sairie and Emily look magnificent in their fancy dresses? That lavender for Emily is perfect and Sairie's cornflower blue matches her eyes."

"Aisling, my love. You look a treat." Aisling's dad stood in the doorway, his heart in his eyes as he looked at his daughter.

"Thanks, Da." Tears sparkled in her eyes. "I'm so glad you're here."

Tom Nuin cleared his throat and crossed to take his daughter's hand. "I'm sorry I couldn't change your mum's mind on this, pet."

"It's okay, Da. You're here, and Emily is here for Gort, and Sairie is here for both of us. Are you ready for this?"

"A man's never ready to give his daughter to another, but little girls grow up, will we nil we, and you're marrying your best friend. There's no better foundation for a long happy marriage." He cleared his throat again and wiped the back of his hand across his eyes. "That's our cue," he said as the music outside swelled.

Laurel picked up her bouquet, squeezing Aisling's hand as she passed, and led the way out the door toward the green path leading to the arbour. Her skirts whispered across the grass, the rustle of Aisling's gown telling her the bride and her dad were right behind her. She paused at the beginning of the aisle between the row of chairs. Garlands of flowers lined both sides and the grass was scattered with rose petals and hawthorn blooms. The music changed and she took the cue to begin her way toward where Gort and Coll waited under the bower. She caught Coll's gaze and concentrated on that rather than on the guests on either side. There were more people seated than she expected, most of them she didn't know. Lily was seated with Stuart in the row directly behind Emily, Aisling having decided she didn't need that many people standing with her and Gort. Sairie stood beside Gort, beaming, and holding her notes. Laurel took her place on the opposite side of Sairie from Gort and turned to watch Aisling and her da proceed up the aisle.

A light breeze wafted Aisling's veil and played with the wisps of hair that escaped the pins. She was the vision of a fairy princess treading softly over the grass toward her true love. Laurel blinked back tears; her gaze caught with Coll's when she glanced toward the men. Gort's attention was only for his bride. His thin, homely face transformed by his love and devotion fairly shone with joy and love. A tear slid down Laurel's cheek at the sight of his overwhelming happiness.

"Who gives this woman to be wed?" Sairie's voice broke into Laurel's thoughts.

"I do," Tom Nuin replied in solemn tones, making no mention of her absent mother. He kissed his daughter on the cheek and took a seat beside Emily who was already dabbing her eyes with a lacy handkerchief.

Aisling handed her bouquet to Laurel and turned to face her soon to be husband. The ceremony blurred for Laurel. She felt Coll's eyes on her but kept her gaze on the flowers in her hands, the petals vibrating gently in her trembling hands. Her friends were so obviously in love, it made her question her feelings for Coll. Did she love him enough to pledge her life to him? Did he love her enough? Now, that was a question she couldn't answer anymore than she could figure out the depths of her own feelings. Laurel dragged her attention back to the matter at hand. She watched Coll hand Gort the ring and he slid it on Aisling's hand, repeating the vows he'd written. Laurel handed Aisling the ring she'd kept on her little finger throughout the ceremony and held her breath while Aisling placed it on Gort's finger and repeated the vows Laurel had helped her write.

"I pronounce you man and wife. You may kiss the bride," Sairie pronounced with a huge smile. The small gathering cheered. Aisling turned with her hand still in Gort's and kissed Laurel as she reclaimed her bouquet. Music swelled as the newly weds led the way down the grassy path toward the reception tent. Laurel fell into step beside Coll, her hand tucked in his elbow. Lily and Stuart came behind, followed by Emily and Tom and Sairie. The rest of the guests trailed after them.

They gathered at a small table at the head of the tent for Gort and Aisling to sign the wedding certificate. Laurel forced her hand not to shake when it was her turn to sign as a witness. She handed the pen to Coll and moved back to let him take his turn. The formalities over, the servers Sairie and Emily had hired moved through the gathering with refreshments and the level of conversation rose around them.

The dinner and speeches went by in a blur, Coll held her hand under the table when they weren't eating. From the corner of her eye, Laurel was aware of Lily glaring at her from her place beside Stuart. She pointedly avoided looking directly at the woman and kept her head tilted toward Coll.

The formal part of the afternoon over, the guests mingled and refreshed drinks while the tables were cleared away for the dancing. Gort and Aisling took the floor for their first dance to the old Cornish song of Hal-an-Tow. It wasn't exactly a love song, but it was one that both Gort and Aisling loved. Coll took Laurel's hand and pulled her out onto the dance floor to join the bridal couple. Stuart and Lily followed with a few of the other guests. To Laurel's annoyance, as the song ended, Stuart tapped Coll on the shoulder and asked for the next dance with Laurel. Which meant that Lily latched onto Coll. She gave Laurel a smug smirk as the music started again.

"Excuse me, Stuart. I see someone I need to talk to." Laurel made a beeline toward her parents who were by the tent entrance. They were talking to someone who was much taller than her dad, which surprised her as Colt Rowan was well over six-foot tall. The gentleman in question tipped his head down toward her mother, the sun striking his blue-black hair. Laurel's heart tripped in her chest, and she hurried her steps. Grampa Vear...could it be...? And if Grampa Vear was here, then where was Gramma Bella?

Laurel looked frantically for Sairie and Emily, for surely if Gramma Bella was here, she would be with those two ladies. She spied a flash of cornflower blue just outside the side door of the tent and changed course. Breathless, she reached the door and stepped outside.

"Gramma!" She threw her arms around her grandmother, almost knocking her off her feet.

"Laurel, little Laurel. Well look at you, girl. All grown up on me." Bella hugged her granddaughter and then held her back at arm's length. "I hear you're quite the little centaur, my love. Riding those big horses over those nasty jumps."

"Hardly a centaur, Gramma. But I love it, the horses, the riding, I love being back in Cornwall. Oh, I've missed you so much." She hugged Bella close again. "Why didn't you tell me they were coming?" she asked Sairie.

"A body can't tell what they don't know," Sairie replied. "It's as much a surprise to me as it is to you."

"Once Vear knew that Colt was here in Cornwall, nothing would do but we make the journey to see him, and you. And of course, the fact it is a wedding of two lovely youngsters makes it all the more enjoyable."

"I saw Grampa V talking with Dad and I didn't want to interrupt them, but I knew you must be here somewhere. I'm so happy to see you." Laurel hugged her gramma again, then broke away and grabbed her hand. "Come say hi to Ash and Gort. I know they'll be thrilled to see you too. I can't believe they're actually married." She pulled Bella back into the tent and looked for her friends.

"Ash! Ash, over here." Laurel waved across the dancers separating them.

Aisling looked up, and then threaded her way between the couples on the floor, a big smile on her face. "Mrs. Rowan, Gramma Bella...oh, I don't know what to call you, but it's so good to see you." Aisling embraced the older woman.

"Why don't you just call me Bella? I'm just Bella now. Mrs. Rowan is someone from another life altogether. Congratulations on your wedding, my pet. Where is that young scamp you married?"

"He's off somewhere with Coll and Stuart. Some secret plan or something." Aisling laughed. "More like they're giving him a hard time about the wedding night."

"You waited until the wedding night to...you know...um..." Laurel headed into uncertain territory.

Aisling's face furrowed into a rueful grin. "Between my mother stalking me before I moved into Emily's and then Emily and Coll being around *all* the time, it hardly gave us anytime to anticipate the wedding night, as my mother would say."

"Oh," Laurel was at a loss for words.

Aisling grabbed her arm. "Are you telling me that you've...you know...with Coll...or Chance? C'mon girl, spill."

"Yes, do tell." Bella grinned and leaned closer.

"No, not that Coll hasn't hinted he wouldn't mind us being more...physical. But it just never felt like the right time." Laurel ducked her head to hide the flush of heat rising from her chest up her throat.

"What about Chance?" Aisling prompted her. "You gotta admit that's one hot cowboy."

"Ash! You're a married woman now!"

"Won't stop me from looking, and answer the question."

"Chance is that Cullen boy if I remember right. Even when he was in diapers, he was your shadow." Gramma Bella smiled.

"Yes, Chance Cullen." Laurel mock glared at both Ash and Bella. "And no, I have never gotten that close to him either. So, if you want advice for the wedding night, I'm not the one to ask."

"Oh," Ash fanned herself with her hand, "I think Gort and I will do just fine without any help. There he is now. I'll see you in a bit." Aisling hurried off through the throng to join her husband.

Gramma Bella took Laurel's hand. "Let's go find your grampa, make sure there's no sparks flying between father and son."

"Yes, of course. I can't wait to see him. I'm sure Mom has things well in hand. Dad's always on his best behaviour when she gives him 'the look'." Laurel giggled.

They made their way toward the main entrance of the tent. Emily and Sairie wandered off to be sure the wedding cake was still intact and ready for the cake cutting. Laurel and Bella stepped out of the tent where the light breeze was a welcome respite from the warmth inside.

"There they are." Laurel pointed toward the pony field where the two tall men were leaning on the fence, Anna Rowan's golden hair a bright counterpoint to the raven hued heads beside her.

"Grampa V!" Laurel lifted the hem of her skirts and hurried across the grass toward them.

"Laurel, my bright love. Look at you, not a little girl anymore, but a young woman now. I'm both proud and sad." He kissed her on both cheeks. "Proud of the woman you've grown into and sad that the sweet child I once knew is in the past. But, I hear you are doing quite well with your equine pursuits. Quite fearless over fences, you are, from the reports I have heard." White teeth gleamed in his olive-skinned face.

"Heard from who?" Laurel caught her breath. Who did Grampa know that Laurel didn't know about?

Vear threw his head back with a throaty laugh. "I have sources everywhere. The elementals keep me up to date on your doing, and the piskies, not to mention the hobs who watch over the barns of Miss Suzy."

"I haven't seen Gwin Scawen much since I've been back. Is he still around here?" Laurel gave a surreptitious glance around her.

"Ah, Gwin. He's been off on some business of mine, but his friends and family have kept watch over you and your friends. I think if you look closely, you will see some of them making sure nothing upsets their beloved Aisling on this special day."

Laurel clapped her hands. "Is that who is making sure Mrs. Nuin isn't going to show up here?"

"None other." Laughter sparked in his dark eyes. "Now, would you be so kind as to favour your old grandad with a dance?" He bowed low and offered her his hand.

"Of course." Laurel giggled. "I'll catch up with you later," she called to her parents and let Vear lead her back toward the tent.

"Where is the ever-loyal Coll Hazel?" Vear asked as he spun Laurel out onto the dance floor. "I thought I would have to beat him off with an oar in order to get a dance with you."

"I don't know. I haven't seen him since just after dinner." She scanned the couple on the dance floor and gathered at the edges. Sure enough, she spotted Coll with Lily, who was pressed as close to him as she could manage. "Looks like he's busy babysitting Stuart's cousin."

Vear swung her through some complicated moves before he replied. "Ah, the ever-present Lily. Yes, I've noticed she tends to cling to him like a limpet. What say you about that?" His sable eyes regarded Laurel.

She sighed and hesitated before responding. "Honestly, I'm not sure. I thought coming back to Cornwall would give us a chance to actually be together and repair the distance that's crept in between us."

"Long distance relationships are always hard." Grampa V nodded.

"It's more than physical distance, though. I never realized that until I saw him again. We've grown up and grown apart at the same time. One minute he's pressing me for a commitment and the next he's running off to hold Lily's hand."

"And this commitment you say he's asking for, how do you feel about that?" Vear led her off the floor as the music changed.

"It makes me uncomfortable if I'm being honest. I like Coll, a lot. But I'm not ready to commit to spending the rest of my life with him...and I'm not sure I ever will be. But I don't want to lose him either."

"Tell me, little love. Do you value him more as a friend or as a lover?" They moved to a quiet corner just outside the tent where the sun was blazing its last orange and saffron light across the land.

Laurel bit her lip and turned his words over in her mind. He waited patiently beside her; face turned toward the darkening sky over Mount's Bay.

"I guess it's his friendship I don't want to lose. I mean, outside of the connections we made when we were younger, we've gone in different directions. We have different interests, and it feels like different priorities." She tipped her head up to gaze into her grandfather's face. "But he's still Coll, and I'm still me, and I don't want to lose him as a friend."

"Perhaps, that is your answer, granddaughter of my heart. I think you know where your future lies, you just need to trust your instincts and follow what your heart is truly telling you, not what you wish it to say. Now, come. Enough of soul searching, this is a joyous day. So let us enjoy it."

"Agreed. Let's go find Mom and Dad and Gramma Bella. It's so special to have all of us together in one place."

Chapter Eleven

"That's the last of it." Coll stacked the last of the chairs into the waiting lorry.

Laurel wiped her hands on her jeans and grinned at Sairie. "Almost back to normal. It didn't seem like all that much work when we were setting things up."

"The clean up is never as easy as the set up. All the excitement is over with and perhaps some of us partied a little too hard last night." Sairie arched an eyebrow at Coll.

"Aye, you might be right about that, but it's not every day that my best mate gets married."

"Off with you, then." Sairie waved the waiting lorry driver on his way.

"I hope Ash and Gort enjoyed everything. It was so nice of Ash's dad and Emily to surprise them with the St. Micheal's room at The Godolphin. It looked amazing when I nipped in yesterday to leave some flowers and bubbly for them." Coll collapsed onto the grass. "God, I'm knackered." He flopped onto his back and groaned.

"Totally self-inflicted." Laurel laughed and nudged him with her toe. "I noticed you gave Lily a ride home last night."

Coll covered his eyes with his arm. "Are you going to give out to me about that? Stuart was bladdered and there was no way I was letting him drive. I got him a ride, but there wasn't room for Lily." He uncovered his face and sat up. "What did you want me to do?"

Sairie snorted and patted Laurel on the shoulder on her way into the cottage.

"You did the right thing. But it would have been nice if you'd taken the time to come and say goodbye before you left." Laurel sank down on the grass beside him.

"Okay, yeah. I guess I should have done that. I was just so crazed trying to make sure everyone got home okay, and nobody thought to follow Ash's dad when he drove them over to the hotel." He turned toward Laurel and took her hands in his. "We need to talk."

"She nodded. "We do. You first."

"Okay, right. I don't want to keep on like this. With you in Alberta and me here. It's just too...I don't know, it just doesn't feel right. Every time I bring up the subject of us making some kind of commitment you change the subject or brush it off. It can't go on like this."

"I know. I know. But I just can't pick up and move here."

"And I can't leave Gramma and move over there. So where does that leave us? You've been here for a few months now. Why can't you make it permanent? I mean things are being taken care of back home, you could just manage stuff from here."

"I couldn't. The only reason things are rolling along at home is because Chance is looking after things for me, but I can't ask him to do that forever. He's got his own responsibilities to take care of."

Coll pulled his hands away and got to his feet. "And there's always Chance, isn't there. Every time I turn around it's Chance this and Chance that. I'm sick of it."

Laurel scrambled to her feet. "That's not true! The only time I mention him is when it's something about the wildies, who are my responsibility, not his. He's been good enough to pick up the slack for me because he knows how important this working student gig is to me. But it's not a permanent thing."

"So where does this leave us?" He scowled at something over her head.

"I don't know," Laurel said miserably. "Can't we just keep being friends? See where it goes?"

"I need more than that, Laurel. I want more than that. If you're not ready to make a commitment, then maybe we need a break. You figure out your feelings for Chance and I'll give you some time to decide if you want a future with me." Coll turned on his heel and strode off toward his car without a backward glance.

"Coll!" Laurel took a step to follow him, her hand raised. She let it fall to her side and stopped as the little car roared down the lane. "Fine. Be like that," she muttered.

"Was that Coll leaving in such a hurry?" Sairie asked when Laurel entered the kitchen.

"Yup." She sank into a chair at the table, chin resting on her hands.

"You two have a spat?" Sairie joined her.

"We broke up. Again. I think." Laurel kept her gaze on the tablecloth.

"You think?"

"Okay, yeah, I guess we broke up. But nothing is ever black and white with Coll."

"Do you want to talk about it, or should an old lady just leave you to brood?" Sairie got up and put the kettle on.

Laurel leaned back in her chair. "Not sure there's much to talk about. He wants a commitment out of me. Wants me to move to Cornwall permanently. Maybe Ash and Gort getting married has put ideas in his head."

"What do you want?" Sairie busied herself wetting the tea.

"I like Coll a lot and I value his friendship. But I just don't know if what I feel for him is love. Or at least enough love to last a lifetime. Does that make me a bad person? I don't think I've led him on."

"No, love. It doesn't make you a bad person. There's love and then there's love."

"What do you mean?" Laurel cradled the mug of tea that Sairie placed on the table.

"I think you know, but if it helps to talk it out...there's the love you have for your parents, and your animals. That's a different love than you have for close friends. But the kind of love you can build a lifetime on is different again. It's all encompassing, an extension of yourself without taking anything away from who you are. It's a sharing and communicating on an almost mystical level. It's not something you can manufacture or make yourself feel." She paused and raised a hand when Laurel made to interrupt her. "Oh, you can convince yourself that what you feel is that deep and abiding kind of love, but my caution is, if you have to convince yourself that's what you're feeling then it isn't real. Those are the unions that end in divorce. Yeah, there was love of sorts, but not that once in a lifetime love. Only you can decide if what you feel is strong enough to last or if it's just the love one friend has for another. Does that help any, my pet?"

"Sort of. It's a moot point right now anyway. He's gone off in a huff, and if I don't miss my guess, he's ranting to Lily right now. I almost feel sorry for the girl." Laurel gulped her tea.

"Perhaps it's best to let things lie for a bit. See how you both feel when emotions aren't running so high. Now, don't you have something exciting coming up soon?"

"The event at Lanhydrock is next week. Suzy is letting me take Blue. It's a smaller one day event and she thinks it will be just the thing to get his confidence back and see how his leg handles the terrain."

"How is our Miriam coming along?"

"Healing. Her shoulder is still giving her fits sometimes, but she's pushing through it. She's coaching me with Blue as she knows him best and she trusts me with him, which is pretty cool."

"Well earned trust I would imagine, love. You've spent a lot of your spare time after work and before nursing that horse."

"It's been awesome. He's such a great horse, not just what he can do athletically, but he's such a good boy. I'm really going to miss him and all the others when I have to go home."

"I'm going to miss you too when you leave. Don't take so long to come back for a visit next time, yeah?"

"Oh Sairie, I'm going to miss you like crazy." Laurel got up and hugged the older woman from behind. "I promise to come visit at least once a year, and then Gramma Bella and Grampa V can show up at the same time. Cross my heart."

"That's a good girl." Sairie patted her hand. "Now let's clear up these tea things and take the ponies for a ride. You don't have to be to work until tomorrow and I fancy a nice hack through the fields and maybe down to the beach at Marazion. How does that sound?"

"Perfect." Laurel gathered up the mugs and gave them a quick rinse. "I'll meet you at the barn, I just have to change."

"I'll tack up Lamorna and Ebony."

"Just bridles, let's go bareback. Then if we decide to play in the water, we won't have to worry about salt stains on the saddles."

"Bareback, it is. Hurry up, then." Sairie's voice floated back into the kitchen as she left the cottage.

* * *

"How are you doing?" Miriam glanced at Laurel. "Suzy really put you and Blue through a workout yesterday."

"I'm good. It was fun taking those tougher options on the cross country. Blue didn't even hesitate in the water."

"I saw. That's good. I was worried she was going to over face you with some of those jumps." Miriam shifted gears and followed the horse van into the roundabout.

"How's your arm feeling? It can't be easy to shift."

"It's feeling better all the time. I can't wait to get back in the saddle and do something besides flat work. You want to go over the course one more time?"

Laurel pulled the crumpled paper out of her pocket and smoothed it on her thigh. "I think I could ride this with my eyes closed. I've gone over it so many times, I dreamed it last night." She laughed. "But it never hurts to take another look."

"Tell me what line you plan to take and why," Miriam put her coach voice on.

Laurel talked her way through the obstacles on the Lanhydrock course, explaining how she planned to approach each one and why, then what line she would take to the next.

"What about your speed. Are you confident you can keep to the required metres per minute to avoid time faults?"

"I think so."

"What are you going to do if you feel like you're behind?"

Laurel grinned. "I'm going to keep moving at a pace that feels right for Blue and me. This is to help Blue's confidence after that fall at Badminton, and it's my first time riding at this level. I'm not going to take any risks that might screw that up."

"Good girl. Trust your instincts, and if Blue feels off at any point just pull up and retire. That shouldn't be an issue, but you never know what can happen when you're on course."

"For sure. Blue and I know each other pretty well now. I'll be able to tell if he's even a tiny bit off."

"I'm just being a mother hen. It's killing me that I can't ride. I get more nervous watching than I ever do when it's me in the saddle." Miriam smiled. "You'll do just fine."

"I hope so." Laurel crossed her fingers.

Sooner than Laurel thought possible they were pulling into the area where the horse vans were parked. Miriam chased her off to get her competitor's bib and check in at the show office. Laurel found it strange to not be the one taking care of the behind-the-scenes things. Miriam assured her that Blue would be unloaded and saddled and ready for her when she returned. Thank God for Miriam, having her as the coach and groom, along with Suzy, took any uneasiness Laurel might have had about Blue's care. Fiona was busy with her own mount today with Vicki grooming for her, which left Janet to run between. Laurel had nothing against Janet, but she didn't fully trust the other girl's judgement or work ethic.

The paperwork taken care of, Laurel hurried back to the horse van clutching her bib and trying to control her breath which kept catching in her chest. Nerves, it was only nerves. She halted beside the cab of the lorry and forced herself to settle down. In a few moments her breathing slowed, and her hands weren't trembling quite as much.

"Okay now. That's better." Laurel walked around the lorry to the van where Miriam and Blue were waiting. Now her nerves were well in hand, Laurel couldn't wait to get in the saddle. This was what she lived for, the joy of sitting on a great horse with a challenge before them. Didn't matter if it was barrel racing or jumping. Dressage was difficult but she never got the adrenaline rush from riding a good test that she did from flying cross country with a willing partner. She ducked into the van and changed into her riding clothes, taking care to wipe off her show boots before slipping them on and tightening the spur straps.

"You look like you're ready to take on the world." Suzy greeted her when she stepped out of the van. "You're third to go in the dressage ring and then third to the cross country start box. Have a good trip. I have to go and give Fee some help with Karma in the warmup ring. We changed her bit and I think we might

147

need to just go back to what she's comfortable with." Suzy hurried off.

"Why'd they change Karma's bit?" Laurel lifted the flap and checked Blue's girth out of habit. Then ran her stirrups down.

"Suzy was worried the mare would be too strong for Fee once she got going. She seemed fine with the kimberwick at home, but she's flinging her head around now. I'm betting Suzy will change back to the snaffle and maybe shorten up the running martingale a bit or add a figure eight. Not for us to worry about, Suzy'll take care of it."

"I'm sure she will," Laurel agreed. She bent her knee and let Miriam give her a leg up into the saddle.

Miriam wiped Laurel's boots with a clean rag before wiping Blue's mouth and the bit. She flicked a bit of dust off his shoulder and stood back. "There, all ready. Get back here after your test as soon as they're done with you so we can change tack and you can change as well."

"I will. Wish me luck." Laurel touched her heel to Blue and the big horse moved off at a sedate walk although she could feel his excitement through the reins and her seat. She leaned forward and ran a hand up and down his neck. "We got this, big boy. God, I can't wait to get out on the course with you. But first," she straightened up and checked her position, stretching her legs down longer with more weight down the back of her leg into her heels, "but first, we need to turn in a credible dressage test with as few penalty points as possible."

The warmup ring was crowded, but Laurel found enough space to practice their transitions and pace in all three gaits. Just for fun, she executed some half-pirouettes and half-pass, even though those movements wouldn't be required at this level. It brought a smile of pure joy to her face, the union of horse and rider. All she needed to do was *think* about what she wanted, and Blue responded to her subtle

148

body movement and weight shifts. It was like she was looking through the bridle with Blue, truly one unit and not horse and rider. She left the warmup when Miriam waved her over.

"You look great. Just remember, don't let him extend across the diagonal, he likes to do that, and this test only calls for working trot." Miriam wiped Laurel's boots again while she talked, then wiped down Blue's bit and mouth and removed any foam that marred his chest. "There, all ready. Just to make things interesting, Suzy is videoing everything and I think I saw your friends here. Someone came by the van and told me they were going to try and stream your ride to your parents."

"What! I knew Suzy was going to video, but I didn't know anyone else was coming to watch."

"Oh, I thought you knew. Well, don't worry about it now. Just go and ride like I know you can." Miriam slipped her hand into the cheekpiece of Blue's bridle and led him toward the area where the dressage test was taking place.

"Have a good trip." Miriam stood back after wiping Laurel's boots and Blue's bit one last time before Laurel rode into the arena to circle the ring while the rider before her cleared the area.

"Do my best." She managed a tense smile before cueing the big grey horse to move forward. The pair circled the outside of the ring, moving from walk to trot to canter and back to walk. "Okay, bud. This is it. Let's try not to mess anything up."

Laurel turned Blue and focused her attention on the imaginary X in the centre of the dressage ring and entered at a smart working trot. The test flowed by, and Laurel allowed herself a huge smile after she executed the final salute and let Blue exit on a relaxed long rein. She ran a hand up and down his neck in praise.

"How was it?" She walked with Miriam at Blue's side toward the van to change the tack, after letting the steward check her tack after the test.

"Well done." Miriam threw an arm around Laurel's shoulder. "A few tiny things to work on at home, but overall, very well done. Suzy will be happy."

Laurel released the breath she'd been holding. She hopped into the van to change for the cross country phase while Miriam stripped off the dressage saddle and the bridle they'd used for the dressage. By the time Laurel was slipping on the numbered bib for next phase, Blue was ready and waiting for her.

"We've got time to pop him over a few fences in the warmup ring before you need to report to the start box." Miriam gave Laurel a leg up and then trotted along beside them toward the dirt ring.

"Are you missing being up here?" Laurel glanced down at her friend and coach. "Is you arm bothering you? You've been doing all the work today."

"It's killing me to have to watch, but I'm thrilled that you and Blue are doing so well. He looks like his old self. Just trust him on the course, he knows what he's doing. My arm is fine, quit worrying about me, you've got a course to ride."

Laurel took Blue over a series of fences in the warmup, revelling in the connection with the big horse. It felt so right and her heart sang. Excitement and adrenaline set her heart racing a bit faster than she would have liked. It took her a minute to breathe deep and control the nerves. After all, this was what she'd come to Cornwall to do. And what a horse to have under her to learn on. It was more than her wildest dreams.

Miriam waved her over and Laurel left the ring and moved to the start box where her number was checked off by the starter. Blue bunched under her, muscles quivering beneath her, his ears pricked forward toward the first obstacle. Laurel forced every other thought out of her mind except the line she wanted to ride. One obstacle at a time, remember to press the button on the stop watch attached to her wrist. Suzy and Miriam told her not to worry about the time, but that it was good practice to get used to keeping track of it while on course.

Then it was time. The starter gave the signal and Blue leaped out of the box at a controlled gallop. At least Laurel hoped it was controlled. The big horse was up in her hand and his stride was bigger than she was used to. Trust him, Miriam's words echoed in her mind. Laurel sat lightly as the grey rose gracefully over the first obstacle and followed the line she dictated toward the next obstacle. She allowed herself a huge smile and forced herself not to yell with exhilaration. This was fun! The water jump was the second to last on the course. Laurel took a bit more hold of Blue as they approached, not wanting him to jump too far into the water before landing. The horse responded to her cues and sat back on his haunches before lifting over the huge log on the bank and splashing down into the water. He didn't hesitate but headed toward the far bank, encouraged by her legs supporting him, and jumped up the bank without batting an eye. Laurel allowed herself a sigh of relief, that was the one obstacle they had worried about after his fall at Badminton. Blue lengthened his stride toward the last fence, they rose together, and then Laurel bent down over his neck and encouraged him toward the finish line. It took a bit to pull him up afterward. Blue was quite ready to keep on going. She brought him back to where Miriam waited at a sedate trot. She slid off his back when they reached her and immediately loosened his girth while Miriam threw a rug over him.

"Well done again, Laurel. He didn't even look at the water, just did his job." Miriam gave Blue a slap on the neck. "Let's get him back to the van and cooled out."

Laurel fell into step beside Miriam and the horse, one hand on his shoulder. "He was perfect," she enthused. "I tried really hard to not tense up coming to the water, but he was so willing, and I don't think he even looked at the far bank. I can't thank Suzy enough for giving me the ride on him today. He's the best horse I've ever ridden."

"You earned the ride." Miriam halted by the van. She and Laurel stripped the tack off Blue and put his head collar on. "We have time before the stadium jumping if you want to go watch." Miriam started to lead the big horse off to walk until he was cooler.

"I can do that if you want, Miriam. Your arm and shoulder have to be sore." Laurel offered.

"Are you sure? I wouldn't mind going over and seeing how Suzy and Fee are making out with Karma. I'll be back before you need to get ready for stadium." Miriam still hesitated until Laurel gave her push.

"Go on then. We'll be fine."

"Back soon." Miriam headed off toward the dressage ring.

Laurel and Blue walked along in companionable silence, the thud of his hooves on the turf almost keeping time with her heart. She started when someone appeared at her elbow.

"Laurel, that was brilliant," Sairie exclaimed, falling into step beside her. "Bloody brilliant. I think I managed to video it, I sent it to your parents. I imagine they'll be calling you once they see it. I'm so proud of you!"

"It wasn't me. This guy is the one you should be proud of." Laurel ran a hand down Blue's neck. "He was awesome. All I had to do was point him in the right direction and get out of his way." She glanced at her watch. "He's cool enough now, I'm going to take him to the van and let him have some water. You coming or are you wanting to watch more of the jumping?"

"If you don't mind, I'm going to go watch. And I need to meet up with Aisling and Gort." She paused. "Coll came along too, and so did Stuart and Lily."

Laurel shrugged. "Figures. Lily never misses a chance, does she? Today is going so well I'm not gonna break my heart over who or what Coll prefers. Not today."

152

"Good girl. I just thought you should hear it from me before they all show up at the van afterward." Sairie gave her a quick hug and hurried off across the grass.

Laurel took Blue back to the van where she let him have a small drink before rubbing his legs down and grooming him. His long tail shone like molten silver in the sunlight and she repaired a few of the braids in his mane that had come askew during the cross country. She offered him another drink and then sat on the fender. If Miriam came back soon, she might run over and watch a bit of the cross country before she needed to get ready for stadium. Blue pulled at the hay in his net tied to the van.

"Laurel! Laurel, are you here?" Miriam arrived, flushed and at a run with Karma in tow.

"Here." She jumped to her feet and met Miriam at the front of the van. "What's wrong? What do you need?"

"Suzy needs you to ride Karma on the cross country. Fee had a wreck in the warmup and she's in no shape to ride."

"What happened?" Laurel pressed a hand to her chest in an attempt to slow the thundering of her pulse.

"Thank God you didn't change yet. Here's Fee's bib. Suzy's letting the officials know there's been a rider change. At this level they're not going to argue about it, especially when Fee is at the medical van."

"Is she badly hurt?" Laurel struggled into the bib and snatched her helmet out of the van, cramming it on her head. "How long before we need to be at the start box?"

"Hit her head, concussion I bet. Maybe hurt her arm, not sure. Suzy sent me on the hurry to fetch you."

"What about Blue? Can we leave him here on his own?" Laurel let Miriam toss her into Karma's saddle. She took a moment to adjust the stirrup length and gathered up her reins.

"I'll bring him along. He's campaigned enough to know how to behave. Now, I want you to take Miss

153

Karma into the warmup and pop her over some fences. She quit on Fee when another rider cut her off. Fee wasn't ready for it and came a cropper. I just want you to see if Karma's confidence is affected and for you to get a feel for her in this atmosphere. You go ahead, I'll catch up with you there."

Laurel nodded and trotted off toward the warmup area. Karma seemed steady and quiet beneath her, responding to her aids without fuss. She ran a hand up the mare's neck and talked quietly to her about nothing. Once in the ring, she circled the perimeter at a trot and canter before turning the mare toward the oxer in the middle of the ring. Karma pricked her ears forward and lengthened her stride as her inner leg took over. Laurel held her firmly with hands and seat, judging her approach. The mare took off perfectly and landed lightly on the far side. She came back to Laurel's aids and took the two uprights set off the track on the righthand side. Laurel pulled her up and joined Miriam just outside the ring.

"She seems fine. No stop in her at all and she jumped a treat." Miriam observed. "I think you'll be fine. You might have to push her a bit more than you did Blue over the cross country, just keep her between your leg and hand. Don't worry about time, just get her around the course cleanly. Pull up and retire if you feel she's sucking back too much. This is her first time at this level and while she's ready for it, the incident in the warmup wasn't in our plans. Trust your gut." Miriam laid a hand on Laurel's leg. Blue pushed his nose into her ribs.

"Thanks, Blue." Laurel laughed. "I think he's giving me a vote of confidence too."

Miriam glanced at her watch at the same time Suzy arrived.

"Time to get you two over toward the start box," Suzy announced. "Fee is going to be fine, a slight concussion and a wrenched arm, but nothing that won't heal pretty quick. The medics are keeping her at the van for observation just as a precaution until we're ready to head home. You ready for this, Laurel?"

"I guess, ready as I'll ever be. Can one of you let Sairie know what happened?" Laurel touched Karma's side and headed toward the starter.

Miriam held Blue back and gave Laurel a thumb's up while Suzy accompanied Laurel to the starter and explained the rider change.

The man gave Laurel a quick smile as he let her into the box. "Have a good trip."

"Thanks." Laurel gave him a grin and then forced herself to think about what line she would need to ride with this horse as compared to what she'd just ridden with Blue. No big changes, except Karma didn't have the length of stride Blue did, so she'd have to allow for that in her approaches.

Karma left the start a bit slower than Laurel anticipated, being used to Blue's initial leap. She gathered her up and added some leg to set the mare up for the first obstacle. Things went better once they were on course, the chestnut mare responding to whatever question Laurel asked of her. She checked a bit coming down the hill toward the water jump at the bottom, setting the mare back on her haunches a bit. The last thing she wanted was to land in the water with the mare on her forehand. Miriam's voice echoed n her head. 'Sure way to get dunked. Don't rush at the water.'

Three strides out from the point that Laurel marked in her head as the takeoff point, Karma sucked back under her. Laurel sat down for a stride and pushed with all her aids. It was one thing to not go too fast, it was entirely another to not have enough momentum to clear the log. The mare responded and bunched her hind quarters under her. She slipped a bit on takeoff and Laurel got out of her way as much as possible to give Karma a chance to recover. A lurch and the groan of the spectators was the only indication Laurel had before Karma landed in the water and floundered. She sought to help Karma keep her footing, but the little mare panicked and threw herself sideways. Laurel just had time to hold her breath before the cold water closed over her head. Pushing away from the horse's thrashing, she got to her feet in the thigh deep water and reached out for Karma. Someone was already in the water with them helping the mare settle.

"Thanks," Laurel gasped, shaking the water out of her eyes.

"Any time, Granddaughter." Vear Du's eyes danced with humour, now the danger was past.

"Grampa! What are...how did...why are you here? Where did you come from?" Laurel thrust her way through the water toward the pair.

"Any time you are in danger near water I'll be there. It's glad I am to see that you're none the worse for wear." He handed her Karma's reins.

"Thanks," she repeated, leading Karma out of the pond. She turned to ask where Gramma Bella was, but her grandfather was no where to be seen. Shaking her head, Laurel squelched out of the way of the next riders.

"Are you okay?" Miriam trotted up beside her. "That could have been a nasty fall. What happened?"

"Did you see that man who caught Karma in the water? Where did he go?" Laurel glanced behind her hoping to see Grampa Vere's tall figure in the crowd.

"What man? I just saw you go for a swim and then you were leading Karma out of harm's way. It looked like she caught a hind leg on the log..."

"Yeah, she sucked back about three strides out and then when I asked her, she responded and I thought we'd be okay." She shrugged. "Maybe I should have pulled up?"

Miriam shook her head. "I probably would have done what you did. I'm not sure you could have stopped without crashing into the log. Don't beat yourself up over this, it happens. This is Karma's first experience on a course like this, it just means we need to do more schooling at home."

They arrived at the van to find Sairie waiting for them. "Oh Laurel, I'm so sorry. I was doing that Facetime thingy with your parents so they could see how brilliant you are, and they saw you go down in the water. I'm trying to get through to them on the phone now to let them know you're okay."

"Dad will be having kittens, but Mom will calm him down. Once I get dry, I'll give them a call." Laurel took the rug from Miriam and tossed it over the steaming mare.

"You go get changed into something dry, I'll take care of her." Miriam pushed Laurel toward the van.

"I can give you a hand, it can't be easy with that sore shoulder still," Sairie offered.

Laurel hurried into the van, glad of the chance to strip off the soaking clothes and wriggle into something dry. Her boots resisted her efforts to peel them off, but they finally came free. Laurel took the time to wipe them down and dry them off as best she could. They were going to require some TLC when she got home. Dry now and with her feet in runners, she jumped out of the van.

Miriam and Suzy were with Karma and the event vet who was checking the mare over. He finished just as Laurel joined them.

"No harm done that I can see. Just maybe a bit of stiffness in the next few days. If it persists, I would advise you to have your regular vet come out and have a look."

"Thanks. We'll do that." Suzy shook the man's hand before she turned to Laurel. "Well, that was a bit more excitement than we bargained for, yeah?"

"I'm sorry, Suzy. Maybe, I should have pulled up, but I really thought we could make it. Are you mad at me?" Laurel's heart was in her throat.

"Heavens no, girl. It was just some bad luck that she caught that hind leg. The takeoff is poached some,

157

and that might be what made her suck back on you in the first place. The more experience the mare gets, the stronger her confidence will get. We've got some work to do when we get home."

"How is Fee?" Laurel took Karma's lead shank from Miriam.

"Fee is fine. I sent her along home with Janet already," Suzy said.

"I'll walk Karma til she's dry then." Laurel made to move off with the horse.

Miriam caught her arm. "You need to get Blue ready for the stadium. Suzy managed to get your spot moved to near the end given the circumstances. But you still need to get changed again and Suzy's gone to saddle Blue. So get along with you." Miriam took Karma's lead shank again. "Did you honestly forget you still have stadium?" Laughter danced in her eyes.

"Yeah, I guess I did," Laurel said sheepishly.

"You and Blue are currently in fourth place, so if you have a good trip in the stadium, you've got a chance to move up." Miriam moved off with Karma.

Laurel lit out at a run. How could she have forgotten about the stadium jumping. What an idiot! Her hands shook while she pulled on clean breeches and shirt. Her show coat was thankfully dry, but shoving her feet into the wet boots was less than pleasant. She bundled her hair up into a hairnet and jammed her helmet on top. A quick glance in the mirror told her she was as ready as she was going to be.

"Ready, Laurel?" Suzy called from just outside the van door.

"Coming," she replied, stepping out of the van to find Suzy with Blue all tacked up and ready.

"You sure you're up for this?" A frown furrowed Suzy's brow. "That was a decent fall you just had..."

"I'm fine," Laurel assured her. She ran her stirrups down, checked the girth, and took the reins from her coach. Suzy gave her a leg up and followed her toward the warmup ring.

"Just go easy, take him over a couple of fences and keep his attention on you. Sometimes Blue doesn't take the stadium fences as seriously as he does the cross country obstacles."

Laurel nodded and trotted into the ring. A couple of circuits at trot just to get her body moving again and focus her thoughts. Then she picked up a canter and turned down the line toward the line of fences. The first was an upright, then three strides to an upright with one stride between it and an oxer. Blue was strong and sure beneath her and rose to the fences with a fluidity that made Laurel's heart sing. She turned left and continued over the higher and wider oxer set on the quarter line of the arena. Blue's ears were pricked forward, and he responded to every one of Laurel's subtle aids. She popped him over the fences a few more times before pulling up beside Suzy.

"Looks like you're ready. Don't worry about the time too much, just try and go clear. This is a schooling event, so I'm more interested in you concentrating on accuracy than speed. You're on deck next, so let's get over there."

Suzy jogged along beside Blue with one hand on Laurel's leg. She whipped out a rag and wiped Blue's bit and face before running a clean towel over Laurel's boots and giving the silver spurs a polish. "Off you go." She patted Laurel's leg and stepped back. "Make us proud."

Laurel nodded and moved into position. The rider in front of her cleared the last fence and the steward allowed Blue into the ring. She frantically tried to recall the order of the fences, and then, with a deep breath, trusted in her memory. It wasn't like she hadn't gone over and over the jump course. It was just like always when her nerves were getting to her. Once she took the first fence, the rest would follow. She halted briefly and saluted the jumper jury. Blue responded eagerly to her aids and surged toward the first jump. Laurel sat lightly, letting him set his own pace. She checked him coming into the big upright and held her breath as the rails flashed by beneath them. A hard left turn brought them to the skinny, then onward to a huge oxer. Yellow rails, she hated yellow rails, but Blue hit the striding perfectly and then they were up and over. Three fences left, Laurel resisted the urge to glance at the time clock. Blue rose over the last three fences and then they were dashing across the finish line to the approval of the spectators.

A huge smile split her face and Laurel leaned forward to hug Blue's neck. Straightening up, they trotted out of the ring to be met by Suzy and Miriam.

"Well done!" Miriam beamed at her.

"He was amazing. What a horse." Laurel couldn't stop grinning. "Thank you for letting me ride him," she spoke to Suzy and started to dismount.

"You'd best stay where you are. They're calling you back into the ring," Suzy advised.

"Oh, I forgot. We're in fourth." Laurel gathered up her reins.

"Actually you're second. Your time beat the one horse in front of you who went clear, and the horse that was in second took a rail. Go on, go enjoy the victory lap." Suzy slapped Blue on the rump as he answered the announcer's call.

The ribbons were pinned and then the music blared while Laurel and Blue followed the first-place horse around the ring in the victory gallop. She grinned at Sairie who was standing right by the rail with her friends. It didn't even bother Laurel that Lily was snuggled as close to Coll as she could get. Laughing, she trotted out of the ring and paused to let Miriam toss a cooler over Blue's back before heading to the van.

It wasn't until they were halfway home that Laurel remembered she hadn't called her parents to let them know she was fine after the dunking with Karma. Still riding the high of the day, she decided it could wait until she got home. Her phone only had one bar at any rate, so it wasn't likely she'd be able to get through until they were back at the barn.

Chapter Twelve

"Coll! What are you doing here?" Laurel pushed away from the sun-warmed stone of the small barn at Sairie's. She hadn't been home from the event for long and was using the excuse of checking on the Fell ponies to take a few moments to savour the positive parts of the day and reflect on the less than positive ones. Like falling with Karma into the water jump.

"I wanted to make sure you were really alright," he paused and looked at the toe of his boot, "but, Laurel, we need to talk." His eyes met hers.

"I'm fine, as you can see. And you're right, we do need to talk." Laurel moved over to the low wooden bench beside the double Dutch doors of the barn. "Things don't seem to be working out quite the way I thought they would."

"Nor for me. I expected we would just go back to the way things were...before...you know..." Coll turned his troubled face toward her.

Laurel laid a hand on his arm. "I know. It just isn't the same. I've got all these responsibilities back home now and that's where Mom and Dad are. I love Cornwall and I love living here with Sairie and being with Ash and Gort and you, but in my heart, I know it can't be forever."

"I wish I could convince you it could be forever." Coll shook his head and covered her hand with his. "It could be forever though. You could just fly back to Alberta a few times a year and that Chance bloke could manage things for you." He met her gaze. "You know he would. Gort and Ash are going to move into his

Uncle Daniel's place once we finish fixing it up. We could live with Gramma after we got married...it would make her so happy and it's brilliant. The house will be mine eventually, anyway."

"Coll, stop and think about this. What were we just talking about? It's not the same between us. We've grown up and apart. The magic or whatever it was is gone but the love is still there." She held up a hand to stop him interrupting her. "The love is still there, but it's the love for a very good friend, it's not the love I could build a life on. And what about Lily? You can't deny there's more than friendship between you, can you?"

He swallowed and looked away, removing his hand from hers. "You're most likely right, but I don't like it and I didn't plan it, and in some ways I wish it wasn't true. I could build a life with you...I could."

Laurel shook her head. "If you're truthful with yourself you'll see that isn't true. You say you love me but there's always been Chance between us and now Lily. You don't trust me, and I can't build a life with someone who doesn't trust me."

"I do trust you!" Coll swung around and stood up to pace in front of her. "I do!"

Laurel leaned on the wall at her back and waited for him to quit pacing.

"Okay, alright, yeah. But it's him I don't trust, not you." He threw himself on the bench beside her, elbows on his knees and head down.

"But if you really trusted *me,* it wouldn't matter to you what Chance did or didn't do because you would know in your heart that it wouldn't have any affect on me."

"I don't get your point, Laurel," he grumbled.

"Okay, then what about Lily? You never mentioned her to me before I came back this spring, but it seems like you've been spending a lot of your time with her. Why didn't you ever tell me? I mean, I yak on about what I've been up to with Carly and Joey. I tell you when I've done something with Chance, usually to do with the wildies or the ranch. But you never even told me you were hanging out with Stuart now, and it would have been easy enough to tell me that Lily was there too."

"I suppose, yeah," Coll grudgingly admitted. "But it seemed wrong to be talking about Lily when we're supposed to be a couple."

"If the friendship was innocent enough, it shouldn't seem wrong, Coll. I don't feel guilty about spending time with Chance because it's usually about business and the few times it's a social thing I always tell you. Chance is a good friend and I've known him my whole life. That isn't going to change, and it feels like you're always letting him stand between us because you can't trust me completely."

"Okay, yeah. I guess I do think about Lily as more than just a friend. I haven't let it get any further than that..."

"Even if Lily wants to?" Laurel supplied the words he was reluctant to say.

Coll shrugged.

"Do you think she can make you happy? Build a life with her?"

"Maybe... I don't know...I haven't let myself think about that." Coll got up and paced again.

"Maybe you should let yourself think about that, then," Laurel said gently. A small bit of her died inside, the teenage dreams of her younger self. She pushed them away knowing with a sudden surety that she was taking the right path. For both of them.

Coll stopped pacing and took Laurel's hands, pulling her to her feet. "I will always love you." He enfolded her in his arms.

"And I will always love you and you will always be one of my best friends." She hugged him back.

Coll swiped the back of his hand across his face before he let her go. "We're good then? We're okay?"

"Always. Now why don't you go find Lily and let yourself think about what you haven't let yourself think about." Laurel linked arms with him and towed him toward the gate where his little car waited on the gravel.

"You're brilliant, you know that? Bloody brilliant." Coll closed the gate behind them and kissed Laurel on the cheek.

"Go on, git." She laughed and pushed him toward the car. Standing back, she watched him turn around and drive down the lane. Long after the car disappeared, she stood staring down the brush lined lane.

Shaking her head, she went into the cottage.

"Got things sorted?" Sairie turned from the sink where she was washing mugs.

"I think so." Laurel dried the mugs on the strainer.

"Everything alright?" Sairie gave her a side-eyed look.

"It will be." Laurel hung up the dish rag, hugged the older woman and headed for bed.

* * *

The next morning found Laurel at work just as the sun was peeking over the hedgerows. She loved the quiet solitude of the yard when it was only her and the horses. It was intimate and soothing. Making her way down the barn she stopped at each stall to stroke the heads poking out and murmur silly words to them.

Soon the barn staff would show up and the place would be full of movement and noise, but for now it was just Laurel and the horses, and the barn cats. She smiled as the big orange tabby twined between her legs.

She went to check on Karma in the far barn after spending a few moments longer with Blue than any of the others. The chestnut mare pushed her nose into Laurel's chest and whuffled through her nose. Entering the stall, she ran her hands over the mare, paying careful attention to her legs, but also looking for tightness or heat higher up in shoulder, back and hind quarters. Satisfied, the mare was none the worse for wear physically, she went to the tack room to see if Miriam or Suzy had posted the assignments for the day yet.

"I'm surprised to see you here this early." Miriam turned from the whiteboard, marker in hand.

"Really? I love it here in the early morning when no one else is around." Laurel went to stand beside her and view the board.

"Yeah, me too. But after yesterday I thought you might have a bit of a lie in."

"Part of me wanted to, but I wanted to check on Karma and spend a bit of time with Blue. I'm going to miss all the horses like crazy when I go home, but him most of all."

Miriam nodded. "Even Suzy has commented on how well you and Blue get along. He's not the easiest horse to ride."

"That's what I love about him." She grinned. "He makes me a better horsewoman and a rider."

"Then I think you'll like today's assignments." Miriam patted her on the shoulder and headed to the office to take care of the mound of paperwork on her desk.

Laurel grinned and went to start the coffee and make sure the kettle was full before the others arrived. Miriam had her down to take Blue for a long hack in the morning and then she was due for a group lesson with Janet and Vicki. Fee was at home recovering from her crash yesterday.

Laurel pitched in with the morning feed, making sure to feed Blue's barn first. She couldn't take him hacking until he'd eaten and had a chance to settle a bit afterward, so she might as well make herself useful.

"What are you doing mucking stalls?" Suzy stood in the doorway of a stall, arms akimbo.

Laurel looked up quickly, afraid Suzy was angry until she saw the humour lurking in her eyes. "Just helping out until Blue digests his breakfast. No point in standing around when there's work to be done." She went back to sifting through the straw for wet spots and horse apples.

"Sometimes I wish I had ten of you." Suzy leaned a hip on the stall door. "Any chance you want to make this a permanent position after your working student stint is over?"

Stunned, Laurel propped the pitchfork against the side of the stall. "Are you talking about a permanent place here?"

Suzy nodded. "You have a natural talent, Laurel. I can promise you the best horses in England to ride and the chance to work your way up to competing at the top levels. If you're willing to work at it and sacrifice a lot of personal things, you could ride at an International and Olympic level."

"I don't know what to say. I'd have to discuss it with my parents and..." she paused and frowned, "would I have to try and get a British passport, give up my Canadian citizenship? Otherwise I couldn't ride for Britain, I'd have to compete under the Canadian flag."

Suzy smiled. "Why don't we cross that bridge when we come it? Let's not go borrowing trouble, as my granny would say. Think about it, talk to your parents and your friends. If you decide to take me up on the offer, brilliant. If not, that's okay too, there will always be horses for you to ride at Longrock. Now finish that stall and then run along and get Blue out for his hack." She pushed away from the stall door, her boots echoing on the barn floor.

Laurel shook her head, having trouble processing the idea of moving to Cornwall on a permanent basis and getting to work with Suzy and ride all the amazing horses in her yard. How would Coll take the news if she decided to stay? The only reason for her contemplating it at all was the opportunity it offered her, being near

Coll didn't even enter into the equation. Could she make him understand that? Their talk yesterday had made one thing clear to Laurel. She loved Coll as a good friend, but it was nothing more and never would be. For that she was thankful he had taken the bit in his teeth and insisted that they have the uncomfortable conversation. The last thing she wanted was for him to think if she decided to take Suzy up on her offer that it could be construed as encouragement for a renewed relationship between them. And what about Chance? Moving to Cornwall would mean not seeing him every day. The thought left a hollow feeling in her stomach.

Finishing the stall, she pushed the confused thoughts from her mind. Blue and a good long hack would help clear her head and maybe, just maybe, make things a bit clearer. The first thing she needed to do when she got off work was video call her parents, she needed to see their expressions when she broached the idea, a phone call just wouldn't do the trick.

With a lighter step, she headed for Blue's tack and brushes. Twenty minutes later, she swung up onto Blue's back and turned his nose toward the bridleway which, if she remembered correctly would take them through some lovely hills and valleys without putting too much strain on the big horse. Laurel let him pick his own way along the grassy path, she reached out plucked some early berries from the brambles in the hedgerow bordering the way. It was easy to let everything slip out of her mind except the rhythm of the horse beneath her, the sky and sun above her and the songbirds serenading her. There was nothing like this back home, maybe if she went to British Columbia, but it still wasn't the same.

The wind was coming from the southwest carrying the faint echo of the surf with it. Sighing with pleasure, she sent Blue into an easy trot and let him break into a rolling canter at his leisure. The horse's long stride ate up the ground and soon she pulled him back to a walk in a sunny green meadow dotted with wildflowers. To her left, the land fell away over the green hummocks of hills where the sea glistened in the far distance. To her right, a shaggy Border Collie cocked his head at her while he guarded his herd of white woolly sheep. If only life could always be this simple. Laurel knew all to well what a foolish wish that was, but still...

"And if wishes were horses, then beggars could ride," she told Blue who flicked an ear back at her as he ambled along.

Laurel pulled out her phone to check the time. They been gone about two hours, time to start wending their way back. She took the next fork in the bridleway that would eventually lead them back to Longrock. The track was even and not overhung with trees, so she urged Blue into a canter, letting the breeze brush her face and lift her hair from her neck. Before the horse could tire, she eased him down to a long swinging trot, letting him stretch his neck long and low, feeling the easy swing of the big back muscles beneath her. Finally, she brought Blue to a walk and encouraged the big horse to amble along at his own pace. Laurel was in no hurry and Blue had the rest of the day off. As long as she was on time for her lesson with Suzy, the morning was her own and Blue's.

* * *

Blue entered the stable yard at a sedate walk. Laurel slid down off his back and ran her stirrups up before loosening his girth. Leading him into the aisle of the barn she took off his bridle by the tack room and slipped on his head collar before fastening the cross ties. She hung the bridle on the four-pronged hook hanging from the ceiling and hurried back out to strip off the rest of the tack. After stowing it on a rack and tossing the numnah into the laundry pile she returned to Blue, brushes in hand.

This was almost the best part of a ride. Putting everything to rights, cleaning any dirt from the hack off

169

the horse and leaving the mane and tail tangle free and shining.

"Laurie! Thank God you're okay!"

Laurel yelped and almost dropped Blue's hind hoof that she'd been cleaning. Straightening and astounded, she whirled to face the unexpected visitor.

"Chance, what the bloody hell are you doing here?" she demanded, one hand pressed to her chest to still the wild beating of her heart. Blue turned his head to peer back over his shoulder at the interruption to his spa treatments.

Chance gulped and snatched the Resitol off his head. "Uh...I was worried about you..."

"What are you doing here? I'm fine as you can see. Why would you think I wasn't?" Laurel went back to cleaning Blue's hooves, happy to have an opportunity to hide her face from him. *What the hell?*

"Colt was in the barn watching the live video from that friend of yours that you're staying with. I saw you get dumped in that lake and then nothing... Christ Laurie, what was I supposed to think? You didn't call your mom or Carly or...or...me... I thought the worst, I mean what if you were hurt bad and I wasn't there—"

"You weren't there to what? Save me? God Chance, what do you think you could possibly do even if I was hurt, which I wasn't." Laurel looked up and scowled at him. "How did you even find me? Who let you into the stable yard?"

"Uh, uh..umm, your friend Sairie...she told me how to get here," he stopped and actually blushed, "she even drove me over here—"

"Where is she now?" Laurel demanded, stepping away from Blue, ready to wring Sairie's neck with her bare hands. She couldn't have at least texted her to give her a head's up?

Chance grinned, although it did look rather strained. "She kicked me out of that excuse of a car she drives and lit out here like a cat with its tail on fire. Told me I was on my own and good luck."

"Hummpf." Laurel went back to brushing the already clean Blue to keep her hands busy while her mind raced in confusion.

"Look, Laurie, Colt and me were watching you jump over those insane fences and then you got thrown in the water with the horse. Lord, you don't know what that did to your dad. He lit out for the house yelling for your mom. She met him on the porch with her phone in her hand. They both tried calling you, but you didn't answer and then they tried calling that Sairie with no luck. They were beside themselves with worry, although your mom had more faith in you than Colt. You know he's never really liked the idea of you galloping all over hell's creation and jumping over things that don't fall down. Let along off cliffs and into water." Chance ran out of breath and had to stop.

"First, I don't jump off *cliffs*, those are just drop jumps. And I couldn't call them because my phone was back at the van, and I had to get checked out by the medics and Sairie was upset and then her phone battery died. I called Mom and Dad when I got home, told them I was fine. Didn't they tell you?"

He ducked his head, colour flaring in his cheeks. "By that time I was already on the first flight I could get to England. I had no idea where you were wasn't close to London. When Colt couldn't get in contact with you, and God Laurie, I kept seeing you going under the water in that lake..."

"Chance, it wasn't a lake, it was a pond, and it was shallow enough for me to stand up in. Didn't you see that?" Laurel put Blue's brushes away and led the horse to his stall, making sure he had fresh water and a flake of hay.

Chance shook his head. "No, the video cut off once you and that horse crashed into the water. Nothing." He spun her around when she shut the stall door and crushed her to him. "God Laurie, all I could think of was what if I'd lost you? I couldn't stand not knowing and waiting around doing nothing. I...I just jumped in my truck and high-tailed for Calgary. Once I got a flight and got on board, I texted Colt to let him know where I was and what I was doing."

"What did Dad say about that?" Laurel's voice was muffled by Chance's shoulder.

"He said good luck and text him once I'd seen you."

Laurel pushed out of Chance's embrace and stared up at him. "Why didn't he tell me that when I talked to him last night? He would have known what you were up to by then?"

"Don't know." He pulled her into his arms again. "You don't know how good it is to see you again and see that you're all in one piece."

Laurel wriggled free again. "I'm fine. Now what are you planning on doing? Where are you staying?" She glanced at her watch.

"Um, well...Sairie said I could bunk there for now. I have to head back day after tomorrow."

"Figures." Laurel shook her head. Trust Sairie to invite him to stay with them. "Look, I have a lesson I need to get ready for. You can tag along if you want but stay out of my way and keep your mouth shut." She jogged off toward the other barn, cursing under her breath. Chance was not the complication she needed right now just after breaking things off with Coll. And then there was Suzy's proposal... She glanced at the sky and grimaced wryly. "Who went and wished me an interesting life," she growled.

"What?" Coll jogged along beside her. "Didn't catch that."

"Nothing, just nothing."

Laurel introduced Chance to Suzy, Miriam and the other girls while she got Chuck ready. The big bay gelding was a bit headstrong but today Laurel welcomed the challenge, anything to keep her mind on the lesson and not on Chance. The young man in question leaned on the rail and watched while Suzy ran them through their paces, then broke the group off into couples, one to work with Miriam and one with Suzy.

An hour later Laurel was hot and sweaty and her thighs and lower back burned. Still, she'd gotten a well done from Suzy and on Chuck that was an accomplishment. Chance hovered nearby while she cooled the big bay out and put him away.

Remembering she hadn't cleaned Blue's tack, she headed to his barn after taking care of Chuck's equipment. To her surprise all Blue's tack was clean and hanging in its place. There was note on the whiteboard from Vicki. *Thought you could use a break today. You owe me LOL Miriam*

"You ready to head home?" Chance lounged in the doorway.

"I guess, unless Suzy has something else she needs me for." Laurel pulled out her phone and texted her boss. Almost instantly the reply came. *Go home you've earned it.* "I'm good to go. I rode my bike over this morning, you want to run behind me?" She grinned at the tall cowboy.

"Nope. Sairie told me to call her when we were ready to leave. She'll be here any minute." Chance looked smug.

Traitor. Seemed like Sairie had fallen for the Cullen charm. If she only knew.... But, Laurel reminded herself, Chance wasn't his father. She went to get her bike as Sairie's car bumped up the lane and came to a stop by the office.

"Ready to go, my loves?" Sairie got out and opened the boot for Laurel to cram her bike in. The front wheel poked over into the back seat.

Laurel gave Chance a speaking look and slid into the passenger seat. She giggled at the expression on his face when Sairie reversed and sped down the lane, barely stopping as she turned onto the narrow road hedged in on both sides with overhanging bushes.

She giggled harder when they arrived at the cottage and Chance crawled out of the back seat on wobbly legs.

"Does she always drive like that?" he whispered to Laurel.

"Pretty much," she replied. "Why?" Laurel batted her eyes innocently.

"Frickin' crazy." Chance shook his head and went to drag the bike out of the boot.

* * *

Later, sitting around Sairie's kitchen table with mugs of tea and plates of biscuits before them, Sairie informed them she had to run into Penzance and pick up Emily for a meeting. Since this was news to Laurel, she gave the older woman a questioning look only to be met with innocent blue eyes with a hint of mischief in them.

"Don't know when I'll be home. You make yourself at home, Chance. Laurel, be nice." With that she flounced out the door and in a moment the headlights of her car swept across the window.

"Laurie, we need to talk, you and me." Chance leaned across the table toward her.

Her stomach knotted. The conversation was eerily familiar to the one she'd just had with Coll the night before.

"Okay, what about?" she hedged.

"You and me, Laurie. You know how I feel about you. I've tried to prove I've changed. Colt and me have had long talks about what I'm planning to do with my life. He's helping me set up a retirement savings plan and everything. Even your mom is on my side."

"That's nice. But I think I have should have some say in this. What about how I feel? And don't call me Laurie!"

"Of course you have something to say in all this. I mean, without you there's...nothing." Chance dropped his gaze to his clenched hands. "Nothing."

174

"That's not true. No matter what I decide, you still have a great future ahead of you and lots of opportunities."

"You're right. But without you in my life it just seems like a lot of empty years. Be honest with me, Laurie. Do I have a chance with you? How do you feel about me?"

"You know you're one of my best friends." She reached out and laid her hand over his clenched fists. "You were such an asshat for so long, it's been hard for me to actually believe you're sincere in the changes you've made. We have so much in common and so many shared memories and Daddy certainly believes in you. But I don't know if I can give you what you're asking for in the long run."

"I know I was an idiot, but I've got my head on straight now and it's going to stay that way. Just tell me you're coming home at the end of June." He turned his hand over and twinned his fingers with hers.

Laurel sighed. "Yes, I'm coming home at the end of June. I got offered a permanent position at Longrock this morning, and while it's really tempting and it would be awesome, I have too many responsibilities at home. The wildies and the ranch. Mom and Dad aren't getting any younger. And don't you dare tell him I said that," she warned. "I'm just not ready to make the sacrifices I would need to in order to accept Suzy's offer."

"Promise me you'll think about what I've said, okay? No pressure, just think about what we could do together." Chance squeezed her hand before his face clouded.

"What?" Laurel prompted him.

"What about that Coll guy? You still hot and heavy with him?" He pulled his hand free and ran his fingers through his hair.

"Coll is, and always will be, a very good friend. But there's nothing more between us. That relationship is over." Laurel clipped her words.

"No kidding?" A brilliant smile lit Chance's face. "And you're coming home the end of June?"

"Yes, and yes." She held up a hand to stop him interrupting. "I promise I will think about what you've said. I'll talk to Mom and Dad about it. I know Dad would be thrilled to know I'd married someone he was confident could carry on the legacy of the ranch. But that's not a good enough reason for me to marry someone."

"Wouldn't want you to marry me just because you thought I was a good manager, Laurie. I love you. I've been an idiot sometimes, but I've always loved you." Chance pushed back his chair and put his mug by the sink. "I'm going to bed. Sairie showed me a room earlier. Night, Laurie."

The door swung shut behind him leaving Laurel gaping after him. Well, that was a different side of Chance than the one she'd expected. No pleading, no excuses, no 'I saw how my dad treated women and I thought that was how a man was supposed to act'. She got up and washed the mugs in the sink, leaving the light on for Sairie whenever she decided to come home, and went up the dark narrow stairs to her room. The light showed under the door of the spare room, and she hesitated. Shaking her head, she went into her own room and shut the door. There was a lot to think about.

Too bad Ash was still away on her honeymoon. It would have been good to have someone like her to talk this out with. Somehow discussing Chance and love with her mom just didn't feel comfortable. Crawling into bed, she turned out the light and laid back to watch the moon shadows chase across the ceiling. A life with Chance could be good. He really seemed sincere. Colt Rowan was a hard man to fool, and Daddy sure seemed to believe in him. Laurel turned on her side and punched the pillow. She picked at her emotions regarding Chance. He *was* handsome, and certainly filled out those Wranglers in a way that caught her attention more than once. He had a good heart, look at the way he'd turned on his father when they were caught up with the dog fighting ring. And he'd put his body between her and bullets when things went bad that night. He'd adopted those scrawny kittens and cleaned the paint off them, always had a treat for Darby, the dog they'd rescued, and Chance had named after the dog his father killed when he was a kid. She had to admit there was more to Chance than she'd given him credit for lately.

A warm feeling cradled her, and she snuggled into her quilt. A life with Chance was a definite possibility. Only time would tell. It was certainly worth thinking about. It was, after all, her choice. And anything was possible.

The End

If you loved this book
(or even just liked it)

Please leave a review...
AUTHORS NEED REVIEWS.
KEEP THIS AUTHOR WRITING.

2021 Bestselling Author
Nancy M. Bell

Nancy lives near Balzac, Alberta with her husband and various critters. She is a member of the Writers Guild of Alberta and the Canadian Authors Association. Nancy has publishing credits in poetry, fiction, and non-fiction. Her work has been included in Tamaracks Canadian Poetry for the 21st Century and Vistas of the West Anthology of Poetry. Her poetry is also being included by the University of Holguin Cuba in their Canada Cuba Literary Alliance (CCLA) program.

BWL Publishing

bwlpublishing.ca

www.ingramcontent.com/pod-product-compliance
Lightning Source LLC
Chambersburg PA
CBHW070033120726
47909CB00003B/1142